THE ALICE BOOKS
by Phillis Reynolds Naylor

The Agony of Alice
Alice in Rapture, Sort of
Reluctantly Alice
All But Alice
Alice in April
Alice In-Between
Alice the Brave
Alice in Lace
Outrageously Alice
Achingly Alice
Alice on the Outside
The Grooming of Alice
Alice Alone
Simply Alice

achingly Alice

PHYLLIS REYNOLDS NAYLOR

A JEAN KARL BOOK

ALADDIN PAPERBACKS

To Jeanie Menz Naylor
and
Julie Holtzman Naylor,
with love and admiration

First Aladdin Paperbacks edition August 1999

Copyright © 1998 by Phyllis Reynolds Naylor

Aladdin Paperbacks
An imprint of Simon & Schuster
Children's Publishing Division
1230 Avenue of the Americas
New York, NY 10020

The Library of Congress has cataloged the hardcover edition as follows:
Naylor, Phyllis Reynolds.
Achingly Alice / Phyllis Reynolds Naylor. — 1st ed.
p.   cm.
"A Jean Karl book."
Summary: Thirteen-year-old Alice sets long- and short-term priorities for her life as she experiences the complexities of young love.
ISBN 0-689-80355-9
[1. Love—Fiction.] I. Title.
PZ7.N24Ac   1998
[Fic]—dc21
97-12430 CIP AC
ISBN 0-689-80595-0 (Aladdin pbk.)

CONTENTS

1. A PROMISING START   1

2. ROOMMATES   12

3. GIVE A LITTLE WHISTLE   26

4. MAKING THINGS HAPPEN   39

5. FEMININE PRODUCTS   52

6. VALENTINE   65

7. PERSUASION   75

8. DECISION   90

9. CONFESSION   103

10. SOMETHING HOPEFUL   112

A Promising start

One of my teachers, Mr. Everett, used to tell us, "Be a person who makes things happen; don't just let life happen to you."

I've been thinking about that a lot lately because I'm starting to plan my life—as much as any life can be planned, I guess—and I wrote down my list of priorities. What do I most want to happen first? That's easy: I want my dad to marry Miss Summers—the gorgeous teacher with the blue eyes and light brown hair.

They've been seeing each other for a whole year now, ever since seventh grade when I invited her to go to the *Messiah* Sing-Along with us. When Dad found out I'd invited my English teacher, he thought she'd be a little old woman he'd have to help down the steps, and was delighted to find that she's intelligent, warm, talented, gracious, beautiful, and, in short, a real sweetheart. She'd make a wonderful wife for Dad and a mom for me, with only one little hitch: Someone else is in love with her, too: Jim Sorringer, our vice-principal.

I'm pretty sure she loves my dad; I've seen the way they look at each other, and they enjoy the same things. It was when Mr. Sorringer took a leave of absence to get his Ph.D. in California that Sylvia Summers and Dad first met, and now that Sorringer's back in the picture, Miss Summers is torn between the two great loves of her life. That's the way I see it, anyway.

The other priorities on my list are:

2. Decide on a career I'd really love, which I *think* is going to be psychiatry, but I'm not sure.

3. Get to know some other guys, even though I really, *really* like Patrick Long.

4. Do something about my body–hair, skin, waist, legs–everything.

5. Be a better sister to Lester and a better friend to Elizabeth and Pamela.

Those are my short-term goals. Marriage and kids and a house and stuff aren't even in the picture yet, but I decided these are the things I should think about first. And since numbers two through five would be a whole lot easier if I had a mother to help me make decisions, I've committed myself to putting all my energy into getting Dad and Miss Summers married.

I used to think I couldn't stand it if they didn't. The thought of having to go through high school, to dances, through breakups and disappointments, getting married, even, without a mom's advice, somebody to talk to late at night about woman stuff, was just too awful. Now, though, I realize that even a mom can't solve everything, but I still want Miss Summers to marry my dad, for his sake. Worse than not having a mother myself is seeing my dad unhappy.

My own mom died when I was in kindergarten. Lester remembers her better than I do because he's seven years older than I am. I keep getting memories of her mixed up with memories of Aunt Sally, who took care of us for a while after Mom died.

I'd already asked Miss Summers if she wanted to go to the *Messiah* Sing-Along with us again this year, and she'd said yes, if she was invited. So I made it official, and Dad was really pleased. Better yet, I found out that Miss Summers invited him, in turn, to the school band concert, the middle of December. But most wonderful of all, Dad announced at dinner one night that Miss Summers was spending Christmas with us.

I gave a yelp of delight and dropped my fork, splattering spaghetti sauce on the front of my sweatshirt.

"Here?" I gasped.

"We could just take her caroling through the neighborhood, if you'd prefer," said Lester.

But I was still staring at Dad. "Christmas Eve and Christmas Day both?"

"I think so," said Dad, smiling.

I leaned across the table and looked him right in the eye. "Where is she going to sleep?" I asked eagerly.

"Al!" said Dad. (My full name is Alice Kathleen McKinley, but Dad and Lester call me "Al.")

"She can always sleep with me!" I begged, pleased that I had a new double bed. What I wanted to know, of course, was whether she would be sleeping with Dad.

"Sylvia only lives in Kensington," he said. "That's about a twenty-minute drive from Silver Spring, as if you didn't know." And then he changed the subject.

I couldn't wait to tell Elizabeth and Pamela at the bus stop the next morning.

"Where is she going to sleep?" they both asked together. I'm not the only one interested in details.

"I don't know yet," I told them. "I'll keep you posted."

For Elizabeth, of course, everyone else's life seems more interesting than her own right now because, after being the only child in her family for thirteen years, her mom's had another baby and, according to Elizabeth, conversations at her house revolve around formula and diaper rash. And Pamela's parents have separated, so she'd rather talk about anything than that.

"Well, I don't think she should sleep over at your house," said Elizabeth. "It just wouldn't look right."

"You're the only one who would be looking, Elizabeth, because you're right across the street," I told her.

With the rush of Christmas events, the band concert came first, and I spent a half hour that day just thinking about what I was going to wear. I'd actually be sitting with Elizabeth and Pamela, but I wanted to be near enough to Dad and Miss Summers that I could see whether they were holding hands.

Patrick, who plays the drums, had a huge drum solo in a

jazz number the band was doing, so I wanted to get there early and find seats on the left side of the auditorium where I'd have a good view of the drums. I told Dad we'd save two seats for him and Miss Summers.

I finally decided on black leggings and a long white sweater. Lester drove Elizabeth, Pamela, and me over early on his way to pick up Marilyn Rawley, his longtime girl-friend. Elizabeth and Pamela, who have had a crush on Lester since sixth grade and were wearing enough perfume to anesthetize a cat, climbed in back.

"Hi, Lester," said Elizabeth. Her voice was high and tight, while Pamela's was just the opposite—low and husky. Lester says that whenever he drives my girlfriends anywhere, it's like carrying Snow White and the Wicked Queen together in the backseat.

I tried to make intelligent conversation.

"Going to a movie?" I asked.

"Yeah, something with Anthony Hopkins in it, I forget what. Marilyn chose it," he said.

Marilyn Rawley works part-time for my dad in his music store, The Melody Inn, and she chooses great stuff for the store's Gift Shoppe.

"Marilyn has excellent taste," I said, and it suddenly oc-curred to me that while I was working to get Dad and Miss Summers engaged, I might as well do the same for Les and Marilyn. I'd *love* to have Marilyn Rawley as a sister-in-law. So I added, probably sounding too much like Aunt Sally, "She could really make a house a home."

"Cut it out, Al," said Lester.

But Elizabeth picked right up on it. We love bugging Lester. "Are you against marriage, Lester?" she asked.

"Let's put it this way," he said. "If I get married, I'm signing on for the whole caboodle—house, furniture, lawn, crabgrass—the works. And I know that as soon as we'd have a house and furniture, we'd think about kids, and with my luck, every kid would be a girl, and every girl would be like Alice, and I would have contributed to overpopulation without providing any socially redeeming benefits whatsoever."

It's impossible to have an intelligent conversation with my brother. I think the reason he dates Marilyn and no one else is that he's too busy with college to make the effort. I mean, getting involved with someone new takes work! Lester knows that all he has to do is pick up the phone and Marilyn will go to a movie with him.

He let us off at the school auditorium, and we were able to get seats about nine rows from the front. We put our coats on the two seats we were saving for Dad and Miss Summers.

They came just before the concert started, and Miss Summers slid in right next to me, with her glorious scent and her glorious shoes and her blue knit dress and mauve-painted fingernails.

I tried to use mental telepathy.

Marry him, marry him, marry him, I thought, directing my vibes her way.

"Almost a full house!" she said, glancing around the auditorium.

Dad could make a house a home, I pleaded silently. *We'd all help! Marry him! Marry him!*

Sylvia Summers focused on me. "How are *you*, Alice?"

"Fine!" I chirped, and if Elizabeth sounded like Snow White and Pamela sounded like the Wicked Queen, I sounded like Tweety Bird. And then I added, "I just *love* Christmas! It's such a . . . a *family* time!"

"It's certainly a time to be with people you love," she said.

Pamela bumped my arm, and I bumped back. All *right*! I thought.

Dad was looking over the program. "I see there's a little of everything–carols, Dixieland, classical, even Haydn. Sounds promising!"

The lights dimmed. Everyone clapped when the band members came out, entering from both sides of the stage in precision formation, one row going one way, one the other. They were all dressed in dark jackets, white shirts, and red bow ties, even the girls. Then the director came out to even louder applause, and the performance began.

I'm the only member of my family who is tone-deaf. I like music, and I hum along with it at home and sing when I'm in the shower and everything, but Dad says I'm singing the wrong notes. That's really embarrassing, because I can't even tell they're wrong. In fact, when I'm running the vacuum sweeper and singing along with the radio, Lester says the vacuum is more melodic than I am.

Elizabeth and Pamela kept whispering about which of the guys were the cutest, but I sat very still because I wanted Sylvia Summers to know that her future stepdaughter appreciates the finer things in life. It was when the band did the jazz number and the spotlight fell on Patrick that I went bananas, and I was the very last one to stop clapping when he was through.

Patrick's a really good drummer. Dad leaned over and whispered to me that he was improvising, which means that the band director just stands there with his arms at his sides and lets Patrick show off on the drums for as long as he wants to. I guess Patrick signaled somehow when he was going to stop, because he began to slow, and after he gave a long drumroll, the director lifted his baton again and the band took over.

Afterward, Pamela, Elizabeth, and I pushed through the crowd to the stage door and went into the band room, where relatives were congratulating their kids.

Patrick saw me and grinned, and I ran over and kissed him right in front of his parents. He's tall, slim, red-haired, and a great kisser.

"You were wonderful!" I told him. "It was really good, Patrick!"

"He *is* good, isn't he?" Mrs. Long said proudly, and Patrick's dad beamed. Mr. Long's a diplomat, and they've lived in several different countries. Both Pamela and Elizabeth hugged Patrick, too, and I noticed there were some other girls standing around, waiting to congratulate him. Patrick's only thirteen, and already he has groupies? I felt pretty lucky to be the girlfriend of the star drummer in school, and wondered why I had even been thinking about getting to know other guys.

We stayed in the band room for a while talking to the rest of the kids who came by–Mark Stedmeister and Brian and Karen and Jill. A new guy at our school, Justin Collier, who was in the band, too, I noticed, and plays the trombone, has been flirting with Elizabeth for the past month. She went over to talk with him.

Finally I remembered that Dad and Miss Summers were waiting to drive us home, so I said good-bye to Patrick and we went around to the foyer, where a dozen or so people were still milling about.

We were just walking over to where Dad and Miss Summers were standing when I saw Mr. Sorringer talking with some parents. He turned and glanced toward Dad and Miss Summers. She guided Dad over in Sorringer's direction.

Elizabeth grabbed my arm and we froze. We all knew what was happening, and we were close enough to hear Miss Summers say, "Ben, I'd like you to meet Jim Sorringer, our vice-principal." Dad and Mr. Sorringer shook hands about as stiffly as if their arms had been mop handles.

"If they were dogs, they would have attacked by now," Pamela whispered.

"A very interesting program!" Dad said to Mr. Sorringer. "I hadn't realized that there was anything but an orchestral arrangement for the Haydn, but it worked very well, I think, for brass."

"Yes, I thought the kids did a great job," said Mr. Sorringer, in his professional voice. He looked at Miss Summers. "And how did you enjoy it, Sylvia?"

Pamela poked me again.

"It was terrific!" she said. "The whole atmosphere was so festive—a great start to the holiday season."

They made a few more polite remarks, and then Dad gently put one hand on Miss Summers's back and glanced around. "Well, we've got three girls waiting for a ride home," he said. "It was a pleasure meeting you, Mr. Sorringer."

"Same here," said the vice-principal.

"They lie through their teeth!" whispered Pamela.

And then Sorringer added, "I'll be talking with you later, Sylvia."

How *dare* he say that! I thought. He just *had* to put in that dig to show Dad he had a claim on her, too, didn't he?

Elizabeth sighed. "I thought when you were grown up you didn't get jealous anymore."

"And the way Sorringer kept calling her 'Sylvia,'" said Pamela.

But I was still feeling awfully good about the evening as we followed them outside. Miss Summers had invited Dad

to the concert *knowing* they might run into Mr. Sorringer.
Dad had put his arm around her to show she was almost
his. And I *think* I saw her slip her hand into Dad's once during the concert.

I wondered if, once they were engaged, I could start calling her "Sylvia." And how long after they were married before I would feel comfortable calling her "Mom."

There were snowflakes in the air–little baby
snowflakes–that disappeared almost as soon as they fell on
our coats, but still, they gave a magical feeling to the night.
A great beginning! I told myself. A promising start! Nice
going for a girl who was about to make things happen.

2

Roommates

There was one little cloud on the horizon. When I asked Dad what he and Miss Summers were going to do on New Year's Eve, he said that, actually, Miss Summers had a long-standing commitment that she didn't feel she could break, so they wouldn't be spending it together. Karen, who works at the attendance desk before school, overheard Jim Sorringer tell the school secretary—an old friend of his—that he and Sylvia would be going out.

I hated Jim Sorringer for that. I hated everything connected with him, even the motherly school secretary who rode with him occasionally to Pizza Hut for lunch. I hated his car and his tie and his fingernails and his office, and became obsessed, almost, with New Year's Eve and the fact that he was celebrating it with Sylvia Summers. I needed to get on with my life, and couldn't as long as I was worried about Dad.

Pamela, Elizabeth, and I talked this over in the cafeteria the next day.

"That's bad news," Pamela said knowingly. "Of all the

days in the year, New Year's Eve is *uno supremo*. You're supposed to save New Year's Eve for the love of your life."

My heart sank.

But Elizabeth wasn't so sure. "Still, Pamela, how can that compete with Christmas Eve and Christmas Day both?"

"And the *Messiah* Sing-Along," I added hopefully.

"New Year's Eve is about sex, though," Pamela told us.

"Yes, but Christmas means family," Elizabeth argued. And then she said loftily, "New Year's Eve is about lust, but Christmas is about love." It occurred to me that for three girls who had spent Christmas with their families for as long as they could remember and had never had a New Year's Eve date in their lives, we were sounding very wise.

"But on a scale of one to ten, New Year's Eve is a ten!" declared Pamela.

"Christmas Eve is an eight, though, and Christmas Day is at least a six, so that makes fourteen," said Elizabeth.

"And the *Messiah* Sing-Along!" I squeaked again. "That's at least a one."

"So there you have it! Fifteen points!" said Elizabeth, and I felt a whole lot better.

Justin Collier stopped by our table. "What's the big discussion?" he wanted to know.

"Math," said Pamela.

He has got to be one of the most gorgeous guys in our whole school, and he finds every opportunity to be near Elizabeth.

13

"Justin," I teased, "if you had to choose, which would you rather spend with the girl of your dreams—Christmas Eve, Christmas Day, or New Year's Eve?"

Justin smiled. "I'd kidnap her around the twentieth of December and be with her for all three," he said. He looked at Elizabeth, and her cheeks turned as pink as her shirt.

Of the three of us, Elizabeth is naturally beautiful, with her dark hair, long lashes, and milky skin. Pamela is pretty in a sophisticated way—she looks best in makeup. Me? I'm half-and-half. I've got fine freckles that disappear under foundation and powder, I've got green eyes and strawberry blond hair, but I need a little lip gloss and blush. We can't all be Elizabeths, I guess.

"Lester," I said that evening, "let's say you had three girl-friends, and you wanted to date them all between Christmas and New Year's. One was your favorite, one was next-best, and the third you didn't like as well as the others, but you didn't want to lose her. What day would you reserve for which?"

"Is this multiple-choice or an essay question?" he asked.

"Entirely up to you," I told him.

"Hmmm," said Lester, putting down his Coke and propping his stocking feet on the coffee table, philosophy book in his lap. "What I'd probably do is book my favorite for Christmas Eve, Christmas Day, and New Year's Eve, and stop by on Christmas afternoon to take my number-two girl some perfume and out to a movie on New Year's Day.

14

Number three? I don't know. A box of Russell Stover candy, maybe, and a promise to call her sometime. Why?"

"No special reason," I said. "I'm just learning about life."

Still, Dad seemed awfully happy that Miss Summers was coming for Christmas, so I got in the spirit of things and helped clean the house. I baked cookies, got out Mom's recipe for scalloped potatoes, pressed our tablecloth and napkins, and helped Dad select the most beautiful Christmas tree on the lot. Then I called Aunt Sally in Chicago.

"Alice, how nice to hear from you! What's the matter?" she said. Aunt Sally always expects the worst.

"Nothing!" I said. "Everything's fine, as a matter of fact. Dad's invited Miss Summers here for Christmas Eve and Christmas Day, and I just wanted to be sure I've thought of everything."

There were ten seconds of silence at the other end of the line. With Aunt Sally, my announcements are always followed by silent meditation.

"Where is she going to sleep?" Aunt Sally wanted to know.

"Now, Sal," I heard Uncle Milt say in the background.

"I'm not sure," I told her.

"Of course it's none of my business, Alice," Aunt Sally said, "but we do have to think of your sheets."

"Sheets?" I said. "We have plenty of sheets."

"But are they clean and pressed?" asked Aunt Sally. "Now

here's what I would suggest, and I assume you're writing this down: flowers, if only a poinsettia; candles for your Christmas Eve dinner; sweet rolls for Christmas morning; and a present for Miss Summers that's neither too personal nor too cheap. Good soap would be perfect."

"Thanks, Aunt Sally," I told her.

"And Alice?" she said. "Once you go to bed on Christmas Eve, stay there."

After I hung up, I tried to figure out what that meant, so I asked Lester.

"She means don't go barging in Dad's bedroom unannounced," he told me.

"I *never* barge in Dad's bedroom without knocking," I said indignantly.

"Well, Aunt Sally would probably prefer that you didn't go near Dad's bedroom at all."

I wonder how sex got to be so important in the first place.

As it happened, Miss Summers came to our house on Christmas Eve with a shopping bag full of gifts for us, but without an overnight bag.

"I've got a Jell-O salad at home in the fridge for tomorrow," she told me, "but I wasn't sure whether you opened your gifts Christmas Eve or Christmas Day, so I figured I'd bring them now."

I was disappointed that she wasn't spending the night with us, and I'll bet Dad was, too, but I suppose Aunt Sally would have been pleased. Still, we had a great evening. At our house we open gifts Christmas morning, but we have our big dinner the night before. I had the table set for five, because Lester had invited Marilyn. Dad had made a rib roast, and the house was filled with its marvelous scent.

All of us had sung in the *Messiah* Sing-Along a week before. I always sit with Dad, who sings tenor, and turn the pages for him, but I don't open my mouth till we get to the "Hallelujah Chorus." Then I join in because it's so loud, nobody can tell that I'm singing off-key.

"Wasn't that fun?" Miss Summers was saying as we all sat down at the table. "I'd always wanted to sing the *Messiah*, but never got the chance, really, till Alice invited me last year. Now I want to make a tradition of it."

I beamed. So did Dad.

"You've got a standing invitation," he told her.

Marilyn and Miss Summers seemed to get along fine, another good omen, because if Dad married Sylvia and Les married Marilyn, they'd be in-laws, too. Marilyn had brought, along with a chocolate pie, English "crackers" to put at each plate—bright little foil-wrapped cylinders. When you pulled the strips at both ends, they snapped, making a popping sound, and broke open to reveal paper hats, trinkets, and riddles—stupid things like, "What did the optometrist say to his assistant?" "You're my star pupil." We groaned. But we all looked festive and silly in our paper hats, which added a lot to the fun.

"Do they still have to memorize poems in seventh-grade

English and recite them out loud to the class?" Marilyn asked Miss Summers. "I remember having to do that. We memorized 'The Raven' by Poe."

"Back in my day," Dad put in, "we memorized 'The Highwayman' and 'Lochinvar.'"

"Well, we still ask students to memorize a poem and present it to the class, but they get to pick their own," Miss Summers said.

I didn't say anything because I remembered the day in Miss Summers's seventh-grade English class when I started to recite one poem but found I was reciting another that reminded me of my mom. And then I cried, right in front of everybody. One of the most embarrassing moments of my life that, somehow, Miss Summers salvaged and helped me survive.

"How about you, Lester?" Marilyn asked. "How did you get through seventh grade without a poetry recitation?"

"I didn't," said Les. "The worst moment of my life, actually. I went to junior high in Chicago, remember, and I chose the 'The Cremation of Sam Magee.' Except that my voice was changing, and every time I said the word 'cremation,' it cracked, and the class, in turn, cracked up. The teacher felt so sorry for me that she let one of the other guys, who had chosen the same poem, recite it with me. That was even worse. Sort of like riding your bike in front of the class with training wheels to hold you up."

We all laughed. Miss Summers tipped back her head, her

hair beautiful and loose around her shoulders, and I couldn't believe Christmas was going so well. Even when our Tennessee relatives called to see how us folks in "Silver Sprangs" were doing and to wish us Merry Christmas, Miss Summers just busied herself in the kitchen.

I hate those calls where everybody in one family has to talk to everybody in another, and you think you're talking to an uncle about the weather when you hear a cousin asking if you've ever had chicken pox.

But Marilyn and Miss Summers put things in the dishwasher while Dad and Lester and I took our turn on the phone, and then Dad put another log on the fire and said whatever dishes wouldn't fit in the dishwasher could wait until morning.

Lester and Marilyn left soon after to make the rounds of friends who were home for the holidays, so I watched the King's College choir in concert on TV, and when Miss Summers took off her shoes, I figured it was time for me to clear out.

I stretched and faked a yawn. "Well," I said, "I think I'll go to bed."

"So soon, Alice?" Miss Summers asked. "It's only ten."

"I always go to bed early on Christmas Eve," I told her. "I used to think that if I lay real still, I could hear sleigh bells, and Mom . . . I *think* it was Mom . . . told me that Santa was on the way."

Dad smiled. "You *did* hear bells, Al."

"Huh?"

He laughed out loud. "I guess you're old enough now to be in on the secret. Every Christmas Eve after you'd gone to bed, I used to take a string of sleigh bells, slip outdoors, and walk around the house, ringing them, so you'd think Santa Claus was coming."

"Ho, ho, ho!" I said, laughing.

"Well, I make a pretty good Santa, don't you think?" asked Dad.

Miss Summers laughed, too, and for just a moment rested her head on his shoulder.

I went up to my room, put on my pajamas and robe, and curled up to read *The Giver*, to the sound of an icy rain against my window. When the phone rang, I tumbled off my bed and answered in the hall so Dad wouldn't be disturbed.

"Alice?" came Elizabeth's voice from across the street. "I see her car's still there!"

"Yeah, but she's not staying over. She's coming back in the morning," I said. "Pass it on."

The wind had really picked up, and the house creaked. This time I crawled between crisp sheets, which I'd put on all the beds, along with fresh towels in the bathroom and clean dishcloths in the kitchen. I liked the thought that our house was cleaner and prettier than it had ever been since we'd moved in, and we were probably as close to having a complete family as we'd ever had since Mom died. When I turned off the lamp, I could see huge snowflakes coming down outside in front of the streetlight. New snow, a new beginning–it just seemed right, somehow.

I could hear footsteps below, a door opening, voices, a door closing, more voices, a TV commentator's voice, and then Dad saying, "Sylvia, I just won't let you . . ."

I crawled out of bed and opened my door softly.

"It's simply too dangerous out there!" I heard Dad say.

And then there was the sound of Lester's voice, accompanied by stomping feet: ". . . ice, snow, then a layer of ice again. We didn't even get to Wheaton. I barely made it out of Marilyn's driveway. The radio said there was a nine-car pileup on the Beltway."

And finally Miss Summers saying, "Ben, I didn't even bring a toothbrush!"

"We'll surely find an extra one around here," said Dad.

"Oh, I just don't know . . ."

"If the lady needs a room, I will gladly donate mine," said Lester.

I was halfway down the stairs in seconds. "She can sleep with me!" I said. "I've got a double bed, Miss Summers, and I put clean sheets on it this morning!"

I couldn't read Dad's face right then, but Miss Summers turned around and laughed. "Okay, it's a deal. I'll bunk with Alice. Ben, I need a pair of pajamas."

"Coming right up," Dad said.

The phone was ringing again, and I tore back upstairs and

grabbed it. Pamela. "Elizabeth says she's still there," Pamela said.

"She is, and she's going to sleep with me!" I whispered excitedly. "Pass it on." And I hung up.

I scurried around my room, picking up underwear and throwing it under the bed, fluffing up the pillows, adjusting the blind. It was like a dream: My teacher, last year's fantastic, beautiful, lovely, glamorous English teacher–my stepmother-to-be–was spending Christmas Eve at *our* house and sleeping in *my* bed!

Lester had put on his boots and gone back outside to start shoveling the steps and walk, but I could hear soft footsteps going back and forth outside my room, a closet door opening and closing, murmurs, and a silence so long that I just knew Dad and Miss Summers were kissing outside my very door!

Then I heard the bathroom door close, water running, Dad's voice downstairs talking to Lester from the porch, footsteps again, and finally the door to my room opened, and silhouetted there in the light from the hallway was Miss Summers wearing Dad's pajamas, the bottoms swirling around her feet.

She tripped on them once, getting across the room, but then slid in beside me. "Well, this is certainly a surprise, isn't it?" she said, bringing her wonderful scent along with her. "This is a storm that nobody saw coming."

"I'm glad, though," I told her.

"Well, I guess we'll have to do without my salad tomorrow, but I think we'll manage," she said. "I usually sleep on my left side, Alice. How about you?"

"Oh, I can sleep any way."

"Good. I wouldn't want to keep bumping knees with you all night," she said, and we both laughed.

Could this really be happening? I wondered. I could think of a million questions I wanted to ask her, but didn't have the nerve.

How could I possibly sleep? What if I kicked in the night? What if I snored or belched or worse? I decided I would be the perfect roommate if I had to lie awake all night long. I would not pull the covers off her. I lay with one hand on top of the blankets to scratch anything that itched above the neckline, one hand beneath to reach stomach and thighs.

"Hmmm," she said, drawing her knees up. "This is a comfortable bed. I'm going to be asleep in two shakes, Alice. Are you?"

"I guess I'm pretty excited—I mean, Christmas and all," I told her.

"I know. But the sooner you fall asleep, the sooner morning will get here. That's what my sister and I used to tell ourselves on Christmas Eve."

"Did you sleep in the same room?"

"The same bed. We were always best friends. I just wish we didn't live so far apart now." She sighed, and I could feel the covers move as she pulled the blanket up around her chin.

This was my last chance, I thought. I might never again have the opportunity to ask her the one question I wanted an answer to. I'd hate myself in the morning if I let this slip away from me. Over and over I rehearsed it in my head: *You and Dad will marry some day, won't you?* If I couldn't ask that, maybe I could say, *Miss Summers, you'd make a beautiful bride,* or, *The only person in the whole world I want for a stepmother is you, Miss Summers.* Finally, when her breathing sounded as though it was getting more slow and steady, I knew I couldn't wait any longer.

"Dad really loves you, you know," I said softly.

But she didn't answer. Her breathing seemed to come from deep inside her chest, and I figured she'd already fallen asleep. I was awake for a long time. I knew an hour went by, maybe two.

Miss Summers began to make little bubbly noises from her lips, like Elizabeth does sometimes when she sleeps, and I decided to try a psychological experiment that I made up on the spur of the moment. It certainly couldn't hurt anything, and just might help.

Moving in slow motion, I turned, inch by inch, and rose up on one elbow. Then slowly, slowly I leaned over my teacher and whispered, "Marry him! Marry him! Marry him!"

All at once I wondered if that was specific enough. What if she was dreaming of Jim Sorringer just then? What if I was encouraging her to marry our vice-principal?

"Jim is a dork," I whispered. "Marry Ben. Jim is a dork.

Marry Ben. Jim is a . . ."

She startled suddenly. "Alice?"

"A . . . a drink!" I said. "I'm going for a drink of water. Hope I didn't wake you."

When I got back, she was asleep again, and I didn't open my mouth for the rest of the night.

I must have slept, because I was aware of waking up. The room was dark, but Miss Summers was gone. My heart began to pound. Maybe it had worked! Perhaps she'd crept out of bed in the middle of the night and crawled in with Dad! Maybe they had been making passionate love and she had told him she had this irresistible urge to be married!

But when I finally rolled over and looked at the clock, I saw it was already morning, and then I smelled coffee from downstairs.

I put on my robe and slippers, combed my hair, went to the bathroom, and brushed my teeth. When I went downstairs, Dad was sitting at the table with his coffee, looking at the snow out the window, and Miss Summers, in her wool pants and sweater, had her feet propped up on his leg. He was caressing one ankle while she ate a sweet roll.

"Merry Christmas!" said Dad. "How'd you sleep?"

"Fine!" I said.

"We make good roommates, don't we, Alice?" said Miss Summers. "She didn't make a sound, Ben, the whole night long."

3

Give a Little Whistle

Christmas wasn't perfect, but it was fun. Having Lester around helped. After eating Dad's breakfast of waffles and bacon, we sat on the floor by the tree and opened our presents.

In addition to one nice gift for each of us, Lester gave us silly little things. For Dad, a small plastic drum with feet; you wound it up and the feet started moving. Lester gave me a lemon lollipop with a bug encased in it, and Miss Summers got a package of brine shrimp; put them in water and they come alive.

I'd bought good soap for Miss Summers, as Aunt Sally suggested, a giant coffee mug for Dad, and a bottle opener in the shape of an eagle for Lester. I received the usual jeans and sweaters and CDs, but all I could think about was whether Dad would be giving Miss Summers a ring.

I had my eye on a tiny box near the back of the tree, and when Dad finally reached for it, I felt my heart leap.

The phone rang.

"Wait!" I said. "I'll get it and be right back." I picked up the phone in the hallway. "Hello?" I said impatiently.

It was Elizabeth.

"Her car's still there," she said.

"I know."

"She stayed all night," Elizabeth gasped. "Did they sleep together?"

"She slept with me," I whispered, and Elizabeth shrieked. "I'll call you later," I said, and hung up.

Back in the living room, Dad and Miss Summers looked at me strangely. But then Dad smiled and handed the tiny box to me. "'To Alice from Sylvia,'" he said, reading the tag.

Trying not to show my disappointment, I gamely unwrapped it and found a small gold whistle on a thin gold chain.

"My favorite uncle gave me that when I was about your age," Miss Summers said. "He used to tell me that if I ever needed him, just 'give a little whistle.' Actually, he and Aunt Elsie were a bit worried about my going out with boys and wanted me to have something for protection if I ever got in a situation I couldn't handle."

I put the whistle to my lips, and a pitiful little squeak came out.

"That's protection?" asked Lester, and we laughed.

But I thought of wearing this around my neck when I went back to school—being able to tell all my friends that it was a gift from Miss Summers—and I leaned over and hugged her. "Thank you!" I told her. "I *love* wearing your things."

Just as Dad reached for another present and placed it on Miss Summers's lap, the phone rang again.

"Sorry!" I said. "Please wait for me!"

I rushed back out to the phone in the hall. It was Pamela.

"Did they sleep together?" she asked.

I knew that Dad and Miss Summers couldn't hear Pamela, but they could hear me. I turned my back on the living room and tried to cover my mouth. "Pamela, I can't talk right now," I whispered.

"What? I can't hear you."

"I'll call you later."

"Don't hang up!" she warned. "Alice, if you hang up, I'll keep calling till you tell me what happened."

"She slept with me," I said, and hung up.

"Is everything that happens in this house being broadcast around the neighborhood?" asked Dad wryly.

I blushed. "No, I've just got weird friends, that's all."

Miss Summers unwrapped the box in her lap. Then she gave a little cry. "Oh, Ben!"

I stared. A book. *The Seesaw Log,* it said on the cover.

"William Gibson's play, *Two for the Seesaw,*" Miss Summers explained to Lester and me. "Ben and I saw the play when we were at the music conference last summer, and I'd heard there was a book about the writing and directing of it—that Gibson had kept a log of all the trials of production—but we couldn't find a copy anywhere."

Dad grinned. "I found it in a rare-books store. Open the cover, Sylvia."

She did, and gave another cry. "His autograph! You found an autographed copy! Oh, you darling!" Miss Summers put her arms around Dad's neck and kissed him, right in front of Lester and me. I wanted to rush to the phone that minute and call Pamela and Elizabeth, but restrained myself.

I realized we hadn't seen yet what Miss Summers was giving Dad. It turned out to be two shirts, a blue striped one and a beige print, with ties to go with them.

"My gift isn't very original, I'm afraid," she said. "Not after that wonderful book."

"I'll think of you each time I put them on," Dad promised, and squeezed her hand.

I sort of wished that Lester and I weren't around. I imagined the passionate kisses that would pass between them if they had the house to themselves. But there was lunch to prepare and the living room to clean up, so Miss Summers and Dad went to the kitchen to cook, leaving Lester and me in charge of the wrapping paper and boxes.

"Lester, I really, *really* thought Dad would give her a ring," I said disappointedly.

"Well, I guess you thought wrong," he said, loading me down with boxes to take to the basement.

"But I had my life all planned!"

"Then unplan it." He gave me another load of boxes, so I couldn't even see my feet. The phone rang, and I dropped them all to answer. It was Elizabeth.

"Well, did he?" she asked.

"What? Propose, you mean? No. He gave her a book."

"A *book*?" Elizabeth said. I could hear her baby brother crying in the background.

"She loves it," I said.

"Was it *Arabian Nights*? The unexpurgated edition?" Elizabeth asked suspiciously. That book had got us in trouble before when Elizabeth secretly smuggled it out of her parents' bedroom and over to my house and read parts of it aloud to Pamela and me on a sleep-over.

"No, a play they saw together once," I told her.

"This is a lousy Christmas," Elizabeth confided. "All Nathan does is fuss."

"Want to come over?" I said.

"*Could* I?"

"I'll call you when we're through eating," I said.

I'd barely taken my hand off the phone when it rang again.

"Are they engaged?" asked Pamela.

"No, he gave her a book," I said dully.

"Oh, Alice!" Pamela said sympathetically. "On a scale of one to ten, ten being the highest, a book, between lovers, is about a three."

"I know. I had such hopes," I told her.

Lester raised his eyebrows.

Pamela's voice grew softer. "Oh, Alice, I'm miserable!" she said. "I'm at Mom's apartment, and her boyfriend's coming over, and I've got to stay until this afternoon. It was the agreement. Dad's at home with Grandma and Grandpa, and everyone's sitting around feeling awful, and I can't *stand* Mom's boyfriend."

"Do you want to come over later?" I asked.

"*Could* I?"

I felt good that we had the kind of home where friends could feel comfortable. I picked up the boxes once more and started for the basement when the phone rang still again.

This time Lester picked it up: "No, they didn't sleep together, and no, they're not engaged," he said. There was a pause, and then I saw his expression change. "Oh, hi, Sal! Sorry! Didn't think it was you. Yes, of course. We had a very nice Christmas!" Lester rolled his eyes at me, and I giggled as I went to the basement.

I had just come up for another load, colliding with Lester's armful of ribbon and wrapping paper, when the doorbell rang.

"What is this, Dulles Airport, Concourse B?" Lester asked.

I went out in the hall and opened the door. There stood Janice Sherman, Dad's assistant manager at The Melody Inn. She's had this giant-size crush on Dad for the last few years, and she was holding a box wrapped in gold foil.

"Merry Christmas!" she said, stepping inside. "I thought I'd drop by with a little Christmas cheer."

I saw Lester pause in the living room.

"Oh!" I said. "How are the roads out there? Miss Summers had to spend the night because she couldn't get home yesterday." It was all I could think of to head her off.

Janice Sherman had started into the living room, but came to a complete stop. "*She's* here?" she asked.

Just then Dad came out of the kitchen.

"Janice! What are you doing out on those roads?"

"They're not bad at all," she said stiffly. "Everything's melting."

"Well, I'm glad to hear that. They were certainly bad last night," he told her.

"Perhaps not as bad as you thought," she replied.

Hoo boy! I said to myself, and made my escape once more to the basement. But when I came up the second time, Dad was saying, "Now, Janice, you know you shouldn't have done this!" and he was holding up a silver ice bucket that had probably cost a fortune. Miss Summers, wisely, stayed in the kitchen, and all I could think of was that when Dad finally *did* propose to Sylvia, they could drink a glass of champagne that had been chilled in this very ice bucket.

Janice left a few minutes later, and we had just sat down to quiche and salad when the doorbell rang again.

"*Now* what?" said Dad.

"I'll get it," said Lester quickly.

I had a big bite of quiche in my mouth when Lester came back in the room bringing Patrick. I swallowed, choked, and had to grab a glass of water.

"Merry Christmas, Alice," Patrick said.

"Mrrrff," I said, coughing again, and Dad patted me hard on the back.

The family took over.

"Pull up a chair, Patrick," Dad said. "We're having Christmas brunch."

"Sure," said Patrick. "I just had breakfast, but I can always eat again." Boys don't get embarrassed about anything, do they?

"Here, Alice," he said. "This is for you." And he handed me a small box.

What was it with all these tiny boxes? I wondered. Was *I* going to get a ring, not Miss Summers?

"I've got your present, but it's not wrapped yet. I was going to give it to you later."

"It's okay. You can give it to me unwrapped," he said, and reached across the table for the quiche.

Miss Summers smiled. "I haven't had a chance to tell you how much I enjoyed your drum solo at the concert," she told him. "How long have you been playing the drums?"

"Forever," said Patrick, with his mouth full.

The thing about Patrick, though, is that he can sound polite even with his mouth full. I think it has something to do with his father being in the foreign service. That's something you learn to do when you're a diplomat.

I opened the box from Patrick. It was another thin gold

chain, and dangling from the middle of it were gold letters spelling ALICE.

"I love it!" I breathed.

"I figured you would," he said, and grinned at me.

"Gold looks good on a girl with strawberry blond hair," said Miss Summers.

I put it around my neck along with the gold whistle.

"What's with the whistle?" Patrick asked.

"It's to wear when she goes out with you, in case she needs help," Lester kidded, and Patrick laughed.

I liked having Patrick there at the table. We finished the meal with him and Lester making jokes and dividing the last piece of quiche.

Later, with Lester outside shoveling again, and Dad and Miss Summers in the kitchen, I sat down beside Patrick on the couch and put my gift in his lap. It was a framed photograph of me that Sam—a guy in our Camera Club at school—had taken *after* I'd stopped wearing green eye shadow. It was a picture I didn't know he was taking. I'd been sitting on the steps outside of school, putting a fresh roll of film in my camera, and had just glanced up when he snapped the shutter.

The teacher used it to demonstrate that sometimes people's eyes get a dead, glassy look when they pose for a picture, but if you can catch them unexpectedly, you get a live, alert look you might not get otherwise.

"Heeeey!" Patrick said, holding it closer and smiling. I

34

could tell he really liked it. "It's a great picture, Alice. It was taken right outside school, wasn't it?"

"Yeah," I said. "Someone from Camera Club took it."

"Was it a guy or a girl?"

"A guy."

"Who was he?"

I looked at Patrick. "Are you jealous? We were practicing portrait shots."

"I just want to know."

"Sam's his name. I don't know his last name."

"He likes you, huh?"

Patrick *was* jealous!

"I hope so," I told him. "I hope a lot of people like me."

That must have been the right thing to say, because Patrick pulled me close to him and kissed me–a light, lingering kind of kiss.

"*I* like you," he said. "A lot."

The fire snapped and crackled, music came from the stereo where Dad had put on *The Nutcracker Suite*, and I could hear Miss Summers talking with Dad in the kitchen. It *was* a nice Christmas, I decided. The only thing that would have made it perfect–if there was such a thing as perfect–would be if Dad and Miss Summers . . . no. If my own mother were alive to meet Patrick. If I could look across the room at my real mother and see if we looked anything alike. Check out her hands, her hair, her smile. I don't know why I missed that so much, but I did.

By the middle of the afternoon, everyone had gone. Patrick's grandparents were coming for dinner so he had to go home, Miss Summers and Dad went to a movie, and Lester drove over to Marilyn's.

I called Elizabeth. "Everyone's gone, and Dad said we could order in pizza. Come over," I said.

"Pamela's here," she told me. "We were just waiting for you to call."

They each came bringing me a present, and I had mine ready for them. We always give each other earrings, only they're not new; we trade our favorite pairs to wear for a year, and then the next Christmas we swap again.

After that they wanted to know what Miss Summers looked like in a slinky black nightgown, and I had to tell them she wore Dad's pajamas, but that was even better.

"He'll never wash those pajamas," said Elizabeth. "He'll want her perfume to linger forever."

Pamela, who was sitting on the floor, leaned back against the couch, her eyes on the fire. "There is no such thing as forever. Not for love, anyway," she said.

"Oh, Pamela, don't say that!" Elizabeth told her.

"All those vows you make when you marry, they don't mean *anything*!" Pamela went on, and her voice broke a little. "Two of my aunts are divorced. One of my grandmothers, even! And now Mom's left Dad, and she's going with this guy who's four years younger than she is and sells NordicTrack. They met in a gym. I hate him!" She turned suddenly and said, "Listen: Let's order the pizza now."

It was only four in the afternoon, but I called Domino's and ordered a pepperoni and onion, a six-pack of Pepsi, and two orders of buffalo wings. A really cute guy from Domino's delivered it, and Pamela tried to talk him into coming inside and having some with us, but he said it was against the rules. He got her telephone number, though.

We sat on the floor around our gigantic coffee table and ate, and Pamela said, "Thanks for letting us come over, Alice. I mean, Christmas and all . . ."

"*Letting* you!" I said. "I need you, too, you know."

We ate quietly for a minute or two. I think we all realized that the pizza and the delivery boy were just diversions on Pamela's part to get her mind off her parents' separation. And finally Elizabeth said, "Here's what I can't understand about love. Why would a man want to go with a woman who would leave her husband for him? I mean, if she could leave her husband, why wouldn't the boyfriend figure she could leave *him* for somebody else?"

"Good question," I said. And then, while we were mulling it over, I added, "Sometimes there's no forever, though, because one of them dies. I mean, I know it has to happen sometime, but Mom was only thirty-nine."

Pamela and Elizabeth immediately put on their pitying faces, and I almost wished I hadn't said anything, because I don't want friends to feel sorry for me just because I don't have a mother.

"Maybe people just change–they can't help it," Elizabeth suggested.

"Sure. One of them buys a NordicTrack and decides to run away with the instructor . . ." Pamela began, and then she put her head on her knees and started to cry.

I put my arm around her from one side and Elizabeth put her arm around her from the other, and we just let her cry awhile. I wished we had a fairy godmother who would swoop into the room just then and make things right. I reached down, took my whistle, and blew.

Pamela lifted her head and stared at me.

"What's that for?" asked Elizabeth.

"Whenever we're in trouble, we're supposed to 'give a little whistle,' and somebody shows up," I said.

"Who?" said Elizabeth.

"I don't know. A fairy godmother or something."

We heard the front door open, and Lester came in.

"Pizza!" he said, sniffing the air, and came over to the coffee table to help himself to a piece. Then he paused, his hand poised at his mouth, and studied us there on the rug.

"Am I interrupting something, ladies?" he asked.

"Fairy Godfather!" Elizabeth joked, holding out her arms toward Lester.

"Just leaving," he said, and went upstairs to his room.

making things Happen

If Christmas was almost, but not quite, perfect, New Year's Eve was the pits.

I hadn't paid much attention to New Year's Eve before. Usually I was too sleepy to stay awake, and–if I did–I'd just stick my head out the window for a minute or two, listen to the horns, and go back to bed.

But now December thirty-first took on a whole new meaning. New Year's Eve meant excitement. Danger, even. To Pamela, it meant sex. It meant the end of something old and the start of something new. What would it mean for Miss Summers, I wondered? Breaking off with Dad and taking up again with Jim Sorringer? Or breaking off with Mr. Sorringer and committing herself to Dad? And what about Patrick and me?

Jill was having a New Year's Eve party, but she'd told us her folks wouldn't be home. So when I asked Dad if I could go and he asked if her parents would be there, I told him the truth. Naturally he said I couldn't go, and I wasn't too disappointed. Elizabeth and Pamela couldn't go, either. I'm not ready for those kinds of parties yet, and besides, I figured I should stay home with Dad in case he got depressed. Or in case Miss Summers changed her mind and came over to spend New Year's Eve with him, instead.

Patrick's folks were giving a party and paying him to be waiter for the evening, and Les, of course, was out with Marilyn and their friends. So Dad built a fire in the fireplace for just the two of us, and we popped corn and played cards till midnight. Then we turned on the TV to watch the stupid ball in Times Square.

If you want my opinion, that is the dumbest thing on TV. I can't understand why people would want to stand around in freezing weather to watch a big silver ball being lowered from the top of a building. That's it. That is absolutely all there is to it, and when it gets to the bottom, everyone goes bananas. There are probably two thousand places I would rather be on New Year's Eve than Times Square.

But when an orchestra began playing "Auld Lang Syne," I kissed Dad and we both got some wooden spoons and metal pie pans and went out on the porch to bang them a couple of times. Tradition. I guess that's about as dumb as the ball in Times Square. Then I went to bed.

I woke up about two and thought I heard voices. I lay there in a half-sleep, trying to decipher where the voices were coming from or whether I'd heard anything at all. I heard a woman's voice, though—then a man's.

Softly I crept out of bed and slipped halfway down the

stairs. The voices were coming from the living room, and my heart leaped at the thought that maybe Miss Summers had ditched Sorringer forever and come back to Dad.

But when I got down far enough, I saw it was only the TV, and Dad was sitting alone in his chair. But he wasn't watching—he had a magazine on his lap and a sheet of notepaper on top. Somehow I knew he was writing to Sylvia. I'd noticed that he wrote her notes and letters from time to time, and I remembered Aunt Sally had told me that it was his love letters that won over Mom after he met her, charmed her away from a man named Charlie Snow. But what kind of a letter did you write to a sweetheart who was out on New Year's Eve with another guy?

He looked so sad—the slump of his shoulders, his rumpled sweater—that I felt like crying. I figured we were both wondering the same thing: What were Miss Summers and Jim Sorringer doing right now, and would she ever come back?

As I went back to bed, I made up my mind: No more waiting for life to happen to Dad. If he wasn't going to make things happen, then I'd do it for him. I couldn't stand the thought of the woman he loved spending New Year's Eve in the arms of another man. What I was thinking about doing was going up to Miss Summers's room at school and telling her something about Mr. Sorringer to make her mistrust him. I'd never done anything like that before, but I'd never seen my dad so lonely, either. The palms of my hands began to sweat. What could I say that would sound convincing?

I was almost afraid to go to school on January second. I worried that as soon as I set foot off the bus, someone would run up and say that Miss Summers was wearing a diamond ring, and I'd know right away it wasn't Dad's.

In my jeans pockets, I was carrying a tube of lip gloss she'd left at our place, waiting until the period just before lunch, when she had her planning session, to take it to her room. I was relieved that I got through the first two periods without any news of Miss Summers, and I told Pamela and Elizabeth I'd see them at lunch.

Then I started up the stairs to Miss Summers's classroom, rehearsing a wild tale about seeing Mr. Sorringer going into a motel with a woman, wondering if I could carry it off. What if she asked the name of the motel? What if she wanted the name of the street? What if she wanted a complete description of the woman?

I could smell pizza coming from the school cafeteria, and suddenly I had this idea. I *had* seen Mr. Sorringer with another woman! It wouldn't be a lie! What about all those times he'd taken the school secretary and some of the teachers to Pizza Hut? Of course, Mrs. Rollins is probably ten years older than he is, and a grandmother, but she'd been in his car, hadn't she?

Before I could lose my nerve, I went on up the stairs and down the hall to Miss Summers's classroom. Just as I'd hoped, she was alone.

"Alice!" she said when she saw me, but my eyes were on her hands. No ring! I felt elated. Empowered!

"Hi," I said. "I just dropped by to return this lip gloss you left at our place."

"I did? I must be getting so forgetful!" she said. "Didn't we have a lovely Christmas, though?"

"I loved it!" I said. "I really liked having you there. Did you have a nice New Year's?"

I may have imagined it, but it seemed as though her eyes searched mine for a moment. "Yes, I did. And now it's a brand-new year," she told me.

What did that mean? That I should expect things to be different? I thanked her again for the little gold whistle and showed her how great it looked, along with Patrick's necklace, against my navy blue sweater. And then I swallowed and said, "Miss Summers, I . . . I just thought you ought to know that I've been seeing Mr. Sorringer with another woman." My voice sounded so high and tight, I wondered if it was mine.

She looked at me quizzically, but didn't say anything.

This was horrible! She *had* to say something! She couldn't just sit there, could she?

"I . . . I didn't know whether to t-tell you or not," I stammered.

"This seems to be upsetting you a lot," she said finally. *Me?* What about her?

"Well, I just thought you should know," I said again. "It's

not the first time I've seen them together, either."

Miss Summers looked thoughtful and toyed with a pencil that slipped out of her hands and rolled off the desk to the floor. "Would it be someone I know, perhaps?" she asked hesitantly, and then I knew she was concerned.

"I'm . . . I'm not sure," I said.

She leaned sideways and picked up the pencil. "Well, you know, Alice, Jim has a lot of friends." She smiled. "Thank you for bringing my lip gloss."

"If I find anything else, I'll bring it by," I said, and quickly left the room.

My heart was beating like a gong, and I had to stop for a drink of water to calm down. Even though everything I'd said was true, I'd told a lie, I knew—a real whopper—but I just didn't feel it was wrong. When your father's life is in danger—his *love* life, anyway—it can't be wrong to try to help him, can it? Dad *deserved* her! He loved her! Didn't somebody say once that all was fair in love and war? At the same time, I was remembering the day I sat in Mr. Sorringer's office telling him that Jill had made up that story about Mr. Everett making a pass at her. Everything Jill had said was true in a way, but it was still a lie. And now I'd done the same thing.

No! I told myself. *It wasn't the same!* Jill had told that story to get Mr. Everett in trouble because he'd given her an assignment she didn't like. I'd told my story about Mr. Sorringer to . . . I swallowed. To get him in trouble because he loved Sylvia Summers. One minute I was proud of myself, and the next I felt like dog doo.

Well, what was done was done. I needed some kind of closure here! I wanted to quit worrying about Dad and worry about me for a change. I decided not to tell anyone about it—not Elizabeth, Pamela, *anyone*. The next few months were the test. We'd survived New Year's, but Valentine's Day was still ahead, and if ever Jim Sorringer was going to propose, it would probably be February fourteenth. If Miss Summers had any doubts at all about Mr. Sorringer, what I'd said should give her second thoughts about marrying him.

At home, Dad was more quiet than usual. I think he talked to Miss Summers that night, because he took the upstairs hall phone into the bedroom with him and closed the door. I could hear his voice soft and low on the other side of the door.

Yes!

I woke up sometime in the night and thought I was sick. I felt cold and shivery, then discovered I'd thrown off my blankets, so I pulled them on again. I was still cold, but I wasn't sick; I was just suddenly aware, in the reality of my bedroom, of the fact that Miss Summers might have seen through my whole scheme and told Dad about it. He'd be furious, no question.

And why did I think she wouldn't ask Mr. Sorringer himself? *What's this I hear about your seeing another woman?* she'd say. In the middle of history the next day, I'd hear this announcement over the school intercom: *Would Alice McKinley please report to the vice-principal?* And there would be Dad and Miss Summers and Jim Sorringer, all sitting there asking me what I'd said and why I'd done it.

I bolted up in bed and moaned. How did I know my lie wouldn't make her insanely jealous and she'd rush right into Sorringer's arms? The best I could hope for, I decided finally, was that Miss Summers would have seen right through me, chalked it up to stupidity, and forgotten about it. But I was in agony all the next day. I was too old to do something like this. Back in fourth or fifth grade, maybe, but not now!

When I saw Miss Summers in the corridor, I turned and went another way. I avoided the hall outside her classroom completely. Finally, when a whole week had gone by and nobody said anything or acted in any way peculiar, I almost decided that maybe it hadn't been such a bad idea after all.

I guess you could say I was feeling unsettled. All of us were—Elizabeth and Pamela, too. There were just too many changes taking place in our lives, and they seemed to be happening too fast.

First, there was this guy Sam in Camera Club who liked me, I could tell. Whenever we went outdoors for photo sessions, he managed to walk along with me.

Next, all of us had changed classes for the second semester of eighth grade, and though I didn't have a single class with Patrick, I had two with Sam—life science and social studies.

And finally, Patrick invited me over for a drum lesson and I found out later his folks weren't home. We'd sat out on my porch once fooling around with a bucket. A radio was playing, and I'd been tapping out a rhythm on the pail. When Patrick noticed, he said I had talent! Then he began drumming on it with me, and we had a pretty good thing going. I may not be able to carry a tune, but at least I have rhythm. He'd been telling me he'd give me a drum lesson if I wanted, and I'd kept putting it off, but finally he called and suggested I come over, so I did. It was after I'd gone down in the basement with him where he keeps his drums that he mentioned his mom was at the dentist.

It wasn't that I didn't trust Patrick, exactly. But ever since he'd grabbed me in the broom closet at the school's haunted house without my even knowing who it was, I'd figured that every so often a guy can go berserk. And if I could walk in Sylvia Summers's classroom and tell her a lie, then Patrick could be expected to do something equally risky.

Patrick sat me down on the little padded drummer's stool, and then he sat on a chair in back of me, his legs on either side, his body up against mine, his hands holding my own from behind, and showed me how to use the drumsticks.

"Hold your left stick between your middle and ring fingers, Alice, and keep the palm up," he said.

It felt awkward, but after a while he had me beating a rhythm on the pedal of the bass drum with my foot and tapping along with my sticks on the snare drum.

After twenty minutes of this, Patrick put on a cassette and played along on the tom-tom, hitting the cymbals with me in all the right places. Sometimes our sticks collided, and we laughed.

It was fun, and I guess I really do have a pretty good sense of rhythm. Patrick thinks so, anyway. But all the while I was doing it, I knew I still didn't want to be a drummer. I mean, it could never be more to me than just a hobby, a fun thing to do, not something I would ever want to do enough to take lessons.

Right then, though, Patrick didn't exactly have his mind on drumming, either, because I noticed after a bit that he wasn't playing anymore. He had his hands on my waist, instead, and his lips were against the back of my neck. He was slowly running his hands up and down the sides of my rib cage, and I felt a *whoosh!* go through my body–like everything was drawing up tight, and my nerve endings were tingling.

"Ummm, Patrick," I said, leaning back against his chest, and this time he bent his head and I turned mine so that we were kissing sideways, full on the mouth, and I felt another *whoosh!*

I lay back in Patrick's arms, and he kissed me again. One

of his hands rested on my chest, and although he wasn't touching my breasts, I think I wanted him to. Then we heard the front door open and his mom's footsteps on the floor above.

I bolted straight up, almost falling off the stool, and Patrick hit his sticks on the drum in a quick roll.

"I'm home!" Mrs. Long called down the basement stairs.

"Okay," Patrick answered. "Alice is here. I'm giving her a drum lesson."

It was quiet for a moment. "Alice is down there?"

"Yes, I just stopped by for a lesson," I called up, not wanting Patrick to get all the blame.

"Well, that's nice," Mrs. Long said, but I think she was just being polite.

We kidded around some more, and after a while Patrick sat on a second stool at the full drum set and let me use the snare. He put on another cassette, and we drummed together this time, me on the snare, Patrick on the bass and tom-toms. It was fun, but I was still reeling from the sensations I'd had when I was in Patrick's arms. I felt wet and tingly, and began to realize I was definitely a sexual being, as Lester would call it. So this is what it's all about, I thought. This is what the little gold whistle was for, maybe.

"Well," I said when the number was over. "I think I'd better get home. Thanks for the lesson, Patrick."

"Hey," he said, grabbing my hand as I stood up. He stood

up, too, put his arms around me, and kissed me again.

When I went upstairs, I said hello to Mrs. Long, and she smiled and said it sounded as though we had a good duet going, and I thought, *You don't know the half of it.*

As I walked home, the hood of my parka up and my hands in my pockets, I figured that Mrs. Long knew very well what had been going on down there. She'd been thirteen once; she must know what it felt like. I have to admit I'm glad she came home when she did, though, because I'm not really truly sure where I would have stopped if she hadn't. I was having feelings I hadn't felt before—terrific feelings that I wanted to feel again. I guess I was thinking that if *this* felt good, I wondered how it would feel if Patrick did *that* and *that*, and . . . well, it was all new to me, and I wanted to talk with someone about it, but I wasn't sure who. Pamela had never put these feelings into words, exactly, and Elizabeth probably wouldn't even know what we were talking about.

I was wrong. The next day after school, Pamela came home with me, and I was thinking about telling her how I'd felt at Patrick's, when the phone rang.

"Alice," came Elizabeth's voice, and I could hear Nathan screeching in the background. "You've got to do something for me. *Please?*"

"Sure. What?"

"I've got to go to the doctor's, and Nathan's really fussy. Mom thinks he's sick, and she's not feeling so good herself.

If I don't go today, though, I can't get another appointment for two weeks."

"And you need someone to go with you?" I asked, making a guess.

"A-Alice, I've got to have a pelvic exam."

"Oh!" I said. "Sure. Pamela's here. We'll meet you outside."

I hung up and looked at Pamela.

"We've got to go to the doctor with Elizabeth," I said.

"What happened?"

"She needs a pelvic exam."

"Oh, my gosh!" said Pamela, and grimly picked up her jacket.

This was it, the thing we had dreaded for as long as we could remember, and it was happening to Elizabeth, of all people.

feminine products

Lester had just come home from the university and was putting his books down in the living room.

"We're going to the doctor's with Elizabeth," I told him. "I don't know what time I'll be back."

"It's your turn to cook tonight, kiddo," he told me.

"I don't care, I've got to go with her. We've both got to go."

"What's she having? A lobotomy?"

"A *pelvic* exam, Lester! Her first pelvic!" I said.

"Oh," said Lester. "Well, tell her to close her eyes and think of England."

"What?"

"Never mind," said Lester.

We went outside and met Elizabeth coming across the street.

"We've got to take the bus to Pershing," she said. "To the medical building."

"You okay?" Pamela asked, studying her hard. "What's wrong with you?"

Elizabeth looked as though she was about to bawl. "Mom *promised* to go with me! It's all so embarrassing!"

"Well, you can tell *us,*" I said.

"It's this . . . itch. You know. Down there. It's driving me crazy. And sometimes I . . . I feel sort of wet."

"Oh, I've had that," said Pamela. "The wet part. You know what it is, don't you?"

Now *I* was curious. "What?"

"The hots."

"Pamela!" Elizabeth snapped.

"It is! When you see a sexy movie or kiss your boyfriend, sometimes you get a little wet. It's normal."

"But the itch . . ."

"Well, if you've got an itch, I guess you should see a doctor," Pamela said. "That shouldn't be too awful."

Elizabeth's face grew redder still. "But a . . . a *man* looking at me down there . . ."

"Oh! A *man*!" Pamela and I said together.

"It's Mom's doctor. She said I probably ought to be going to him now. Oh, guys, I'm so scared!"

I put my arm around her shoulder as we waited for the bus. "I don't know if this will help, but Lester said—"

"You told *Lester*?"

"I just said you were having a pelvic—"

"You told Lester I was having a *pelvic*?" she screeched.

"He knows you have a pelvis, Elizabeth. Relax," Pamela told her.

"He knows I've got an *itch*?"

I thought she might pass out.

"All I said was that you were going to the doctor to have a pelvic exam, and he said to tell you to just close your eyes and think of England."

Elizabeth blinked. "Why?"

"It's what he said."

"What's England got to do with it? They don't have pelvics in England?"

"I don't know. He's weird. Forget it," I told her.

We crammed in together on the back seat of the bus, one of us on either side of Elizabeth, and to make her feel better, tried to think of things she *could* be going to the doctor for.

"What if you were going to the doctor to have a foot amputated?" I tried. "You would gladly go through a pelvic instead, Elizabeth, and it wouldn't seem like such a big deal."

"What do feet have to do with it?" Elizabeth said irritably. We obviously weren't helping at all.

"I've heard of girls who have to go to the doctor because they get to be eighteen and still haven't had their periods," said Pamela.

That was a new one to me.

"So what does the doctor do?" I asked. "Puncture their . . . ?" And then, when Elizabeth moaned, I said, "Listen, we've been through a lot together, and we'll get through this." I was desperately fishing around for a change of topic.

"Do you remember when I moved here from Takoma Park?"

Elizabeth smiled a little. "Yes. Mom and I sat out on the porch watching the movers take stuff in, and Mom said, 'Well, Elizabeth, it looks as though you'll finally get a friend your own age.'"

"And you brought over our dinner that first night," I reminded her.

Elizabeth straightened up suddenly. "And you were so *rude*, Alice!" She laughed a little.

I laughed, too. "That's because Dad had promised to take us to Shakey's for pizza that night, and then I knew we wouldn't be able to go. We had to eat your meat loaf, instead."

We all started laughing.

"I wanted Miss Cole for a teacher that fall, but got Mrs. Plotkin," I went on. "I even tried to get Mrs. Plotkin to kick me out of her class so I could have Miss Cole. And then, I ended up really loving her."

"She had a heart attack, you know," said Elizabeth.

"I know. I went to the hospital to see her," I said.

Thinking about Mrs. Plotkin in the hospital got us thinking about doctors again, and Elizabeth took a deep, quavery breath and stared straight ahead.

The bus stopped at the corner of Georgia and Pershing, and we walked the few blocks to the medical building. We took the elevator to the second floor and went through the door that said GYNECOLOGY. Elizabeth signed in at the desk.

Then we sat together on the vinyl couch and pretended to look at *People* magazine.

"I'm going to ask him if he can prescribe something without looking at me," Elizabeth mewed plaintively. "If I just tell him how it feels, maybe he can give me some medicine."

"If he could do that, you could have just talked to him on the phone," I said. "Besides, there are probably a lot of different things it could be, and he won't know which it is without examining you."

Elizabeth whimpered again.

"You could always just poke a hole in the sheet," said Pamela.

"What?" cried Elizabeth.

"The sheet. It's made of paper, you know. Just tell him to tear a little hole down there, and then he won't see anything except what he absolutely has to."

Elizabeth shoved her away. "That is so obscene, Pamela! That's awful!"

"So I was just trying to be helpful," Pamela said, but I think she was beginning to enjoy the whole thing. It was our chance to find out what a pelvic was like without having to go through it ourselves.

"Maybe the nurse could look and tell him what she saw," Elizabeth said hopefully.

"And miss his chance?" Pamela teased. "Why do you suppose he became a gynecologist in the first place? *Think* about it, Elizabeth. Of all the things this guy could have been, he chooses a job where he spends the whole day looking at naked women."

Elizabeth closed her eyes.

"Oh, Pamela, shut up," I said. "*Somebody* has to do it."

"I know, but doesn't it make you wonder?"

I began to wish we'd left Pamela home, and was sure of it when I realized that Elizabeth was breathing too fast. Hyperventilating. I was about to suggest we get up and walk down the hall when a nurse came out of the examining rooms and walked over.

"Elizabeth Price?" she asked. "Now I wonder which of you girls she could be?"

The one who was breathing through her mouth with her eyes closed, who else?

"She's a little scared," I said.

"Oh, I'll be right with you the whole time," the nurse told her, taking her hand, and Elizabeth rose to her feet like a Christian going to the lions.

"Think of England," Pamela whispered after her as Elizabeth followed the nurse through the door.

"What do you suppose that means?" I asked, and we both tried to figure it out.

"Maybe it has to do with all the queens who were be-headed, and you can be glad the doctor is working on you down there and not up by your neck," Pamela suggested.

All we could really think about was Elizabeth, though,

and what was happening to her. Now she was probably taking off her clothes . . . Now she was climbing up on the examining table.

I didn't want to think about it anymore. I grabbed the magazine again, and Pamela and I kept turning the pages, but neither of us was reading.

When twenty minutes had gone by and Elizabeth still hadn't come out, Pamela turned to me. "You don't suppose she's pregnant, do you?"

"*What?*"

Pamela shrugged. "You can never tell. Mom said that when she was in high school, the girl everyone thought would never marry was the first one down the aisle, and that of all the girls in her senior class, it was a minister's daughter who got pregnant."

"But if Elizabeth's pregnant, who would the father be?" I asked.

"With Elizabeth, it would probably be an Immaculate Conception," Pamela quipped.

Now I was *certain* we should have left Pamela home.

It was another ten minutes before Elizabeth came out. She looked like a zombie. She was clutching a prescription and stared straight at the door as she walked directly across the waiting room. We had to grab our jackets and hurry to catch up with her.

"Elizabeth?" I said out in the hall. "Is everything all right?"

She kept walking and pressed the button for the elevator.

"What happened?" asked Pamela.

Elizabeth turned and faced us: "I have just gone through the worst embarrassment of my entire life."

"It was that bad?" I croaked.

The elevator came and we got on. The door closed.

"You wouldn't believe how awful," she said, leaning against the wall and closing her eyes.

"Well, *tell* us, so we'll know!" I pleaded. "Sooner or later Pamela and I will have to go through it."

"First," said Elizabeth, "you have to take off everything from the waist down."

Somehow that seemed worse than taking off everything.

"In front of the doctor? Like a striptease?" asked Pamela.

"No!" Elizabeth was horrified at the thought. "Of course not! They give you a paper sheet, just like you said, to wrap around you, and then you get up on an examining table and the doctor comes in, and then . . ." She covered her face with both hands.

"No matter how awful it is, we have to know," I told her.

"The nurse asks you to lie down and put your feet up in these stirrup things, and then you have to wiggle down until your bottom is right at the edge of the table." Suddenly Elizabeth started to cry.

Pamela and I stared at each other in horror.

"And then . . . ?" Pamela asked tremulously.

"The d-doctor sits on a little stool right between your legs, and they lift up the paper sheet and turn on a light." Elizabeth sobbed. "I kept my knees together and finally the nurse had to come over and hold them apart."

I realized that I had covered my face, too, and we were all standing there, hardly breathing. Nobody had pushed the button, so the elevator hadn't moved.

"Then . . . ," said Elizabeth in anguish, "he looks."

I couldn't believe this. "H-He just turns on a light and looks?" I bleated. "He just sits there like he's watching television?"

"Well, he's examining you . . ."

"And he doesn't say anything? Just looks and examines you?" Even Pamela was horrified.

"Oh, he's talking the whole time. He tells you exactly what he's going to do next, and the nurse is chattering away about how it doesn't seem possible that it's a brand-new year already, did I go out on New Year's Eve and kick up my heels? And all I can think about is that my heels are practically up on the doctor's shoulders that very moment!" She sobbed loudly. "I will never go to a doctor again, I will never have a baby, I will never let a man look at me like that! I just can't stand it! I'll die if I ever have to do that again!"

"Did it hurt?" I asked in a small voice.

Elizabeth wiped her eyes and blew her nose. "No. But then the nurse left the room, and he said I could sit up. He wanted to talk, and I couldn't even look him in the face. He wanted to know if I had any questions."

"Ha! I'd ask why the nurse left the room!" said Pamela.

"Since I didn't say anything, he said that I had a vaginal discharge, and that's what was making me itch. And then he said . . ."

Somebody on the first floor must have pushed the button, because the elevator started to move.

"He said *what,* Elizabeth?" I asked.

"Wait till we get outside," she told me. "This is the *really* embarrassing part."

I wasn't sure I wanted to hear it. What could be more embarrassing than lying on a table with your feet in the air and a doctor sitting there *looking*? But I was beginning to feel something else: that Elizabeth was enjoying telling us. For the first time in her life, *she* was telling us something that *we* didn't know.

Once we got downstairs, she had to turn in the prescription at the pharmacy, and then we sat on a bench along one wall to wait.

"*What?* What did he say?" Pamela and I asked together.

"He said sometimes you have a discharge because you have a slight infection, and other times it's just a hormonal thing–that . . . that you get wet because you're sexually excited, and that was normal."

"See? I was right! You get the hots!" said Pamela. "Boys get a hard on, and girls get the hots."

"And he *also* said," Elizabeth continued, and we waited, "that some girls touch themselves down there, and that's normal, too. That can make you wet, but masturbation can't hurt you."

I'd heard the word before and was pretty sure I knew what it meant, but what I couldn't believe was that Elizabeth had said it. Did *Elizabeth* touch herself down there, too? I wondered. There were some things even we didn't ask each other.

"I have to put on some kind of ointment and I'm going to douche," Elizabeth said.

"To *what*?" I asked. I was learning all kinds of things I'd never heard before.

"Rinse out your privates," Pamela said knowingly. And then she added, "Mom says almost no one does that anymore."

"But I feel so gross!" Elizabeth told us. "I itch and I'm smelly and I'll bet all the boys can smell me, and that's probably why I was the last one chosen on a volleyball team in gym today."

I couldn't believe my ears. "Elizabeth, *I* don't smell anything, and Pamela doesn't smell anything, and the only thing we smell in gym is sweat. We *all* sweat."

"I don't care. Even dogs can smell me. I walked to the mailbox yesterday, and this retriever came right up and sniffed. I was mortified! I told the nurse I felt gross, and she said if it would really make me feel better, I could douche, so I am."

We sat silently contemplating our womanhood.

"I'll bet doctors get so used to examining women that

they don't even think about it after a while," Pamela said.

"Yeah," I agreed. "I'll bet it's no different to them from lifting the hood of a car and doing a tune-up."

"Or opening the oven to see how a roast is doing," added Pamela.

"They might even be thinking of baseball scores while they're examining you," I chirped hopefully. "And besides, we can always choose a woman doctor, you know!"

"Yes!" Pamela and Elizabeth said together, and somehow the future seemed a lot more hopeful than it had before.

After we got the stuff from the pharmacy and went back to my place, we went up to my room to see what was in the sack. There was a tube of ointment and a little white plastic pouch that held a rubber tube, a long nozzle, and a soft plastic bag that looked like a hot water bottle.

"That must be the douche," Pamela guessed.

We stared at the contraption while Elizabeth read the directions:

"Attach nozzle to the hose, the hose to the bag, and fill bag with very warm water. Lie down in tub on your back, insert nozzle into vagina, and hold until the bag is empty."

Elizabeth wasn't about to douche in front of us, but we had to see how the thing worked. We had to know everything there was about being a woman. So we went into the bathroom, put the nozzle on the hose and the hose on the bag, put the opening of the bag under the faucet, and turned on the water.

Instantly a stream of water began spraying all over the bathroom.

"Shut it off! Shut it off!" I cried.

"Hold the bag lower!" yelled Pamela.

"No, hold the nozzle higher!" I shrieked.

In the confusion, Elizabeth disconnected the hose from the bag and water poured all over the floor. We all screamed.

Lester tapped on the door.

"Al, do you suppose I could use the john?"

Elizabeth shrieked again.

"Just a minute!" I told him.

I grabbed the bath mat and mopped up the floor, Elizabeth slipped the douche bag under her shirt, and we all traipsed out of the bathroom, dragging the hose behind us.

"Ladies?" came Lester's voice.

We turned, and he gallantly handed us the nozzle and closed the door.

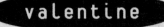

valentine

Womanhood was getting too complicated for me. It must be so much easier for guys, I thought. Girls are just plain messy.

I told that to Dad as we were mashing potatoes for dinner. Every so often we have what he calls *real* food. We don't just mix up powdered potatoes, we actually boil them and mash them with milk and butter.

"Not any messier than boys," Dad said. "Boys ejaculate, you know. We always figured you couldn't get much messier than that."

"But I'll bet it's a lot easier for boys to be examined than it is for girls. Lester said to tell Elizabeth just to close her eyes and think of England, but it didn't help. We didn't know what he meant."

Dad laughed. "It's been said that back in Victorian times, that was the advice brides-to-be got from their mothers on their wedding nights."

"I don't get it," I said.

"Well, back then women weren't supposed to get any

pleasure from sex. They were told it was something they just had to endure, so brides were instructed to put their minds on something pleasant–England, for example–while the act was going on."

That was about the stupidest thing I'd ever heard. We go our whole lives wondering what sex is all about, and when it finally happens we're supposed to think of England?

Dad yelled for Lester to come to dinner, and when he sat down at the table, he said, "Have the screaming meemies gone home?"

"You weren't supposed to come in the bathroom, Lester," I told him.

"I didn't. I knocked."

"Well, you sure picked a bad time."

"Sorry, but it's the only bathroom in the house." He helped himself to the roast chicken.

"We were just looking at the stuff Elizabeth got from the drugstore," I explained, and then, just as Lester lifted a fork to his mouth, I added, "She has to douche." Oh, I love bugging Lester!

His eyes rolled upward. "Do you mind, Al?"

I just kept at it. "And she has to use ointment because she has a slight infection." I remembered a commercial I'd seen on TV. "A *yeast* infection," I added knowingly.

"You're excused, Al. You can leave the table anytime," Lester said.

I took some mashed potatoes and green beans, and went

right on as though I were talking only to Dad: "The doctor said there are at least three things that can cause wetness down there."

"Dad?" Lester said pleadingly.

"Oh, I think I can stomach this all right, Les. It's instructional, after all," Dad told him.

"Hormones," I said, "infections, and masturbation."

Lester dropped his fork.

"Problems, Lester?" I asked pleasantly.

He reared back in his chair. "She just *does* that, Dad. Comes out with stuff that no civilized person would talk about in public," Lester complained. "We're raising a social ignoramus here."

"This isn't public, and I'm just curious," I said. "Do men ever itch down there?"

"You've heard of jock itch," Dad told me.

"And do they . . . ?"

"Yes. *Now* can we have an ordinary conversation, do you think?"

Lester shoveled down his food as though he wanted to finish dinner before I opened my mouth again. But I was quiet for a while. I was thinking about Pamela, actually.

"I'm worried about Pamela," I said finally. "She's really having a hard time of it since her mom walked out."

"You've been a good friend to her for a couple of years now, honey. Just keep on being a good friend," Dad said.

"It's so sad, though. She's sad, her dad's unhappy, and

her mom's dating this NordicTrack instructor. If someone could just get through to Mrs. Jones about how ridiculous she's acting . . . "

"Well, don't let that someone be you," Dad told me. "The last thing in the world you should do is get involved in her parents' love life. It's up to them to work it out. Just be there for Pamela when she needs you."

I wished he hadn't said anything about the love life of adults. It had been more than a week since I'd told Miss Summers that lie, and I wished now it had all been a bad dream. Valentine's Day, though, was right around the corner, and somehow I felt that if I could only get Miss Summers past that without her getting engaged to Mr. Sorringer, we were beyond the danger point.

There would be a Valentine's dance at school, only it wouldn't be formal or anything. Most of the kids just come in groups, and everybody goes home together—not like the eighth-grade semi-formal that was held each May. That would be my first school dance in a long dress. The bad part about the Valentine's dance was that some of our school band members had formed a combo to play for us. Patrick would be the drummer in the combo, of course.

Justin Collier made a point of asking Elizabeth if she'd be there, and Patrick asked me, but a lot of good that did me.

"That's not fair, Alice!" Pamela said sympathetically. "Patrick will be playing most of the evening. What are you supposed to do?"

"Just hang out with you and Elizabeth, I guess," I told her. Not only was Patrick playing in the combo, but he would be leaving the dance early to catch a late flight to Vermont. He and his folks were flying up there for a three-day ski trip. I wouldn't even see him after the dance.

"You know what? We need a life," Pamela said. "I'm sick of boys and I'm sick of Mom. Of school. My hair is awful, and my face is breaking out."

"Yeah, tell me about it," I said.

Pamela and I called each other a lot. The fact was she could have had a dozen boyfriends, but she'd broken up with Mark Stedmeister to date Brian, and then she broke up with Brian to go back to Mark, and she even went out a few times with my old boyfriend back in Takoma Park, Donald Sheavers. But what Pamela needed was nothing a boyfriend could give her. So she'd talk and I'd listen, and lots of nights she called me just to connect with somebody. We'd sit and do our homework together over the phone until Dad came by and made me hang up. I think it was the night we were on the phone together watching TV that Lester freaked out, though.

"You're not saying a word!" he yelled.

"We talk during the commercials," I told him.

He grabbed the phone out of my hand. "Lester to Pamela; Lester to Pamela," he said. "This phone is out of order until further notice. All messages for Alice may be delivered on foot or by mail. I repeat: This is not a working phone." And he hung up.

"You're horrible!" I told him. But at least we'd already worked out what we were going to wear to the Valentine's dance. Since the seventh-grade girls were talking about wearing red-and-white polka dots or pink-and-white lace, we eighth-grade girls would come in black, a bunch of us decided—sophisticated black, with bright red lipstick and nails. Show them how it's done!

On February fourteenth, I opened my locker at school to find this huge one-pound chocolate Hershey's Kiss wrapped in silver foil waiting for me. LOVE FROM PATRICK, it said on the tag. It made me feel warm and happy inside. I wished I could divide that feeling and share it with Pamela.

She and Elizabeth both came over to my house that evening, and Pamela had this white, white face powder that we all put on, so that our eyes, lined with mascara, really stood out. So did our lips.

"Yikes!" said Lester when he put on his jacket to drive us to the school. "What are they? The three witches from *Macbeth*?"

"We're gorgeous, Lester, and you know it," I said.

When we went out to the car, we saw that Lester had already picked up Marilyn for their Valentine date, so the three of us squeezed in back.

"My, don't *you* look elegant!" Marilyn said, turning around.

"*See,* Lester?" I told him. And then, to Marilyn, "Where will you guys be going?"

"Oh, there's a club over in Bethesda we like–good music, good food. We're going to meet some friends," she said.

When we got to the school and were walking up the sidewalk, Pamela said, "I can't understand why Lester and Marilyn would be spending Valentine's Day with friends! I mean, the whole *point* is to be alone with your sweetheart! The point is to make love!"

"That's all you think about, Pamela! Sex, sex, sex! Just *doing* it, like animals!" Elizabeth snapped.

Even I was surprised.

"Well, aren't *we* touchy all of a sudden!" said Pamela. "What do you have against bodies, Elizabeth, other than the fact that you hate pelvics?"

"It's just that you're so one-sided! When you get married, sex is only one small part of it, you know," Elizabeth said.

"Well, darn!" Pamela joked. "What's the rest?"

"Babies, diapers, cooking, cleaning, shopping, babies . . . "

"You already said babies," Pamela told her. "Anyway, I'm never getting married." And even though she was still joking, she sounded as though she meant it.

All at once I grabbed Pamela's arm with one hand, Elizabeth's with the other, because there, going in the door ahead of us, were Mr. Sorringer and Miss Summers. *Together!*

"Relax," said Pamela. "Maybe he just gave her a ride, that's all."

"But she could have brought Dad!" I insisted.

71

"Maybe she figures that she's still on the job at this dance. You know, chaperone and everything. She probably doesn't consider it a real date," Elizabeth suggested.

That was possible.

The combo was already playing when we got inside, and we put our coats on the coat tables and went into the gym. The word had spread about wearing black, because almost all the eighth-grade girls were in it. We really stood out among the ruffles and hearts of the seventh-grade girls and felt very grown-up. I had on a black sweater and leggings, Pamela was wearing a long black rayon dress with thin, pointy-toed boots, and Elizabeth had on black pants and a black lacy top.

"You girls look so sophisticated!" Miss Summers said, greeting us at the door to the gym.

"Happy Valentine's Day," I said, trying to smile.

"Thank you, Alice. Have a good time," she said.

I absolutely refused to say, "You, too." I did not want her to have a good time. I wanted her to have a perfectly miserable time—to look at Jim Sorringer's craggy face and wish she had brought Dad instead.

"Gentle Ben," she had called him once. How could she not love my father more than any other man in the world?

I moved through the crowd toward the combo there on-stage so I could wave to Patrick, but before I could get there, I heard a voice behind me.

"Hi, Alice."

I turned and saw Sam. He is slightly on the chubby side, but he has nice eyes, a nice smile. And I like him.

"Dance?" he said, nodding toward the patch of floor where the couples were doing a fast number.

I'm not sure what I thought I would be doing all evening while Patrick was playing, and since you couldn't tell who was dancing with whom, anyway, I said, "Sure," and followed him over. We shook our bodies and moved our feet. Patrick caught a glimpse of me, smiled, and added a couple extra beats on the drum to say hello.

I milled around with Pamela and Elizabeth after that, walking through the halls with the other girls, gathering in the restroom to talk, taking our Pepsis out on the steps and watching some of the guys horse around. Patrick spent as much time with me as he could. Whenever the combo took a break and they put on a CD, Patrick came over and danced with me. So I was having a pretty good time.

But later in the evening, I was standing at the edge of the dance floor when Sam asked me to dance again, and I did. This time, though, when the fast number was over, the combo went immediately to a slow one, and the lights dimmed. Without even asking me, Sam put one hand on my waist and held my other hand, and we started to slow dance. I guess when you tell a guy you'll dance with him one number, he just assumes you're good for two.

I don't even know how to slow dance–only a waltz with my dad–but Sam is a good dancer. He placed his hand firmly on my back so that I could tell which way we were going to go.

It seemed strange to be holding another guy's hand after going with Patrick for so long, my left hand on Sam's shoulder. I expected him to feel pudgy, but there was more muscle than fat. His face is round, maybe that's why he looks chubby. Actually, he was looking pretty good right then.

We were dancing out of Patrick's line of vision, and I was glad, because I really didn't know how to handle this. To break away from Sam right then would have seemed awfully rude. If I didn't like him, I shouldn't have agreed to dance with him the first time. On the other hand, I wondered what Patrick would think. How was I supposed to get to know other boys, though, if I was always worried about what he'd think?

Sam didn't try to press against me or anything. The point was . . . well, I *liked* dancing with him. I liked his quietness. He reminded me a little of my father. It was all so confusing.

And then it was as though my world came to a stop right in front of my eyes, because Sam had slowly turned me around to dance in another direction when I saw—not ten feet away—Mr. Sorringer dancing with Miss Summers. They were dancing the same way we were, except that Mr. Sorringer's cheek was against Miss Summers's, and though her eyes weren't closed in ecstasy or anything, she was smiling.

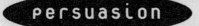

persuasion

Dad went to bed shortly after I got home–Elizabeth's dad picked us up–and didn't even ask if Miss Summers was there, so I didn't tell him. He'd been working on income taxes, and when Dad's doing taxes, he has a one-track mind.

I couldn't sleep, though. I was still wide awake at two o'clock when I heard the front door close, and Lester's footsteps on the stairs. I got up, pulled on my robe, and stuck my head in his room.

"Lester . . . ?" I whispered.

He jumped. "Ye gods, Al! Don't hiss at me. You sound like a snake."

"Could I talk for just a minute?" I went on in and closed the door. Lester was taking off his shoes, so I sat down beside him on the bed.

"I saw something horrible tonight," I began.

He glanced at me quickly. "Accident, right?"

"Worse."

He waited.

"Mr. Sorringer and Miss Summers were dancing cheek to cheek at the Valentine's dance."

I could see Lester's shoulders slump with relief, but I could tell by his face that it wasn't the best news he'd ever heard, either.

"It just isn't *right,* Lester! The way she was with Dad at Christmas—how can she go do something like that!"

"Is that all they did?" he asked, trying to sound matter-of-fact.

"Probably not," I sniffled. "Probably at this very moment, while Dad's sleeping peacefully in his room, Mr. Sorringer is over at Miss Summers's house helping her take off her black lace slip with the slit up one side."

"Whoa! You even know what kind of underwear she owns? What do you do? Snoop?"

"I saw her buying it once."

"Well, neither of us knows what's happening between her and Mr. Sorringer, Al, so it makes no sense to guess. But just because a man and a woman dance cheek to cheek doesn't mean they've got something going."

"It doesn't?"

"No. I can remember when high school teachers came to dances with their wives and sometimes they exchanged partners and danced cheek to cheek. But it doesn't neces-sarily mean they were trading bed partners."

Did you ever notice how one word can suddenly add an-other crack to your nice, peaceful view of the world?

"Necessarily?" I squeaked, and stared at my brother. "Lester, are you telling me that those high school teachers *probably* didn't, but *could* have been, trading wives?"

"Well, it's been done."

"You mean . . ." I gasped. "I'll trade you a blonde for a brunette, or a fat for a skinny, as though they were baseball cards or something?" I was horrified.

"Al, I didn't say it *happened*."

"And when the wives who got traded went to the other wives' houses, they put on the first wives' nightgowns and . . ."

"Will you shut up?"

I just couldn't take any more. I got dramatically to my feet. "If this is your world, Lester, I don't want it," I said, and marched toward the door. But I stubbed my toe on the foot of his bed and collapsed against the wall, holding my toe and sobbing.

Lester put his hands on my shoulders and guided me over to his desk chair to recover.

"Some people automatically kiss friends when they meet, Al; some just naturally hug; and some feel very comfortable dancing cheek to cheek with anyone they happen to be with. In most cases, it does not mean, 'Let's jump into bed and make mad love.' Okay?"

I swallowed. "But it *could*?"

"Anything is possible in this world, but that doesn't make it probable."

I *would* have to have a philosophy major for a brother. But at least it helped me get to sleep.

It was the Monday after the Valentine's dance that I got the news. I was sitting in history when Pamela walked breathlessly into the room, handed the teacher her pass, and said she had to speak to me in the hall about an emergency.

The teacher looked at her skeptically, but said I could leave the room briefly.

I quickly got out of my seat and followed Pamela into the hall. She led me away from the open door, then grabbed my arms. "Guess what? Karen's dad owns that jewelry store on Georgia Avenue, and one of the clerks told her that Mr. Sorringer came back after Valentine's Day to return a diamond."

My mouth dropped and my eyes opened wide. "*What?*" I grabbed her by the shoulders and we both jumped up and down.

"It worked! It worked!" I cried gleefully.

"What worked?" asked Pamela.

I stopped jumping. "Just . . . just having her at our house for Christmas and everything," I said.

The teacher came to the door.

"Miss McKinley?" he said.

I hate it when teachers call you by your last name.

"Coming," I said.

Pamela went back to her class, and I felt as though I were flying. For once in my life I had done something impulsive that had actually paid off. Every time my conscience reminded me that I had lied, I told myself I'd done it for Dad. He deserved her more than Mr. Sorringer did. If Jim Sorringer had really loved Miss Summers, I reasoned, he wouldn't have gone off to California for his Ph.D. without marrying her first and taking her with him. It was while he was gone that I'd introduced her to Dad. If she married Dad, I'd devote the rest of my life to keeping her happy to make up for the lie.

The hardest part was not telling anyone what I'd done. As soon as Lester got home from his class at the U, I grabbed him and swung him halfway around.

"I saved this dance for you?" he quipped. "I thought you wanted me to stop the world and let you get off."

"Not anymore!" I said. "Something wonderful happened! Well, actually, something awful *didn't* happen, and that's the wonderful part."

"You had a test and could have flunked, but didn't," he guessed.

"Mr. Sorringer bought a diamond for Miss Summers and she turned him down. He returned it to Karen's father's jewelry store. I can't *wait* to tell Dad!"

"You will *not* tell Dad!" Lester said sternly. "You've got to keep out of their love life, Al! How many times have I told you that?"

"But what harm will it do? He'd love to know."

"Because one would assume that if it's all over your

school, Dad already knows about it, and if he'd wanted to share it with us, he would have told us. If he doesn't know about it yet, he would be devastated to think that Sylvia didn't tell him herself—that he had to find it out from you."

That made sense. Elizabeth called and we talked about it some more, and I said, "That just goes to show that couples can dance cheek to cheek and it doesn't mean they're trading bed partners."

There was silence from the other end. *Uh-oh,* I thought.

"*What?*" said Elizabeth.

"Trading bed partners," I said meekly.

"You mean . . . adultery?" she said.

"I guess so. Exchanging wives for the night. Lester told me about it."

"Alice, I am never getting married! Never, never, never, never, never, never, never!" she wailed.

"Me either," I said, and we hung up.

Five minutes later, when she recovered, she called back and remembered what she'd called me about in the first place. "When are we going to work on that commercial?" she asked.

We were studying persuasive techniques in social studies, specifically commercials. How some were informative and useful, and others were heavy on fear mongering and misrepresentation of facts. The teacher had divided the class into six sections of five students each, and each section had to write and perform a commercial. Our group was composed of Elizabeth and me, Sam, Brian, and Jill.

"I don't know," I told Elizabeth. "You want us all to come over there?"

"Brian called and suggested we meet at your place. It's hard to do stuff here with Nathan crying."

"Okay, tell him to come at eight and call Sam. I'll call Jill," I said.

Lester had gone to a basketball game at the U with some of his buddies, and Dad said of course we could practice here. He seemed in a pretty good mood. A *very* good mood, in fact, and I couldn't help but think that he knew all about Miss Summers and Mr. Sorringer. I gave him every opportunity to tell me when I said, "Well, *you* look like you got some good news today!" but all he said was, "That new clarinet instructor at the store is working out fine."

I was brushing my teeth around seven-thirty when the doorbell rang. I *hate* it when people come early and you're not ready. What if I'd been in the shower?

"I'll get it!" I called to Dad, and clattered downstairs, wiping my mouth on my sleeve. I opened the door, and there stood Patrick.

"Patrick!" I said. "You're back! How was Vermont?"

"It was okay," he said, but I'd never seen him look so serious. "Well, are you going to invite me in or not?"

"Sure! Actually, a bunch of kids from social studies are coming in a half hour to practice a commercial. You can stay if you want."

He stepped into the hall and looked at his watch. "I'll be gone," he said. "I just wanted to know if you'd had a good time at the dance."

He'd seen!

"Yeah, I did. The music was great. Everyone liked the combo," I said.

"How about Sam? Did he like it?"

I didn't answer, and Patrick said, "I asked someone who you were dancing with, and he said Sam Mayer. I'd never noticed him before, but I guess you had."

"He's sort of quiet. He's in Camera Club," I told Patrick.

"The guy who took your photo?"

"Yes. Listen, Patrick, he asked me to dance, and what else could I do? You were onstage playing."

"That's my fault?"

"Patrick, what are we arguing about here? It's nobody's fault for anything. It was just a dance! I wasn't exchanging bed partners or anything."

"*What?*" said Patrick.

I leaned back against the wall and closed my eyes, wondering if Dad was hearing all this from out in the kitchen. How did life get to be so complicated? If Elizabeth didn't run off and join a nunnery, maybe *I* would!

"You like him?" Patrick asked, and his voice was a bit softer.

"Of course I like him. I like a lot of kids. I also like you, in case you didn't know."

Patrick reached out, clasping my shoulders, and kissed me—a light, hesitant sort of kiss—and then he just studied my face. "Um . . . Crest," he said, licking his lips. I wiped my mouth again, and we laughed. "All right," he said. "See you around."

I watched him leave. I liked the long, lean look of him. I liked the way he usually knew what to do in public, his self-confidence. But I also liked Sam's quietness. His smile.

Is this what Miss Summers was going through? I wondered, except about one hundred times worse? I guess when you settle on one person, there are always things you have to give up. I had to admit I liked having two boys interested in me, yet it didn't stop the sinking feeling that I was supposed to choose.

When the other kids arrived, Brian and Sam had already written a draft of the script. Brian sort of took over as director. We had to demonstrate the different ways a commercial could be misleading, and would be graded according to how many of these we worked into the script: faulty correlations, incomplete data, fear engendering, appeal to vanity, and creating unreasonable expectations.

Dad said hello to everyone and retreated back to the kitchen where he was baking bread.

"So what have you got so far?" I asked Brian as he handed each of us a copy.

"Boy meets girl, conflict, boy gets girl," he said. "That's it."

"What's the product?" Jill wanted to know. I was afraid

for a moment, knowing Brian, that it would have something to do with Jill's large breasts, because they're very obvious, and she's obviously proud of them. In fact, I had nightmares that the commercial would start out with Elizabeth saying, "I wore a 32A cup bra until I tried Ex-pand," and Jill would take her place and say, "And now I look like this."

"The product," said Sam, pulling a tube of toothpaste from his pocket, over which he had taped, in black letters, THE WHITE STUFF, "is 'The White Stuff'–the *right* stuff. Teeth whitener."

We laughed.

"All you have to do is use this whitener on your teeth and you'll have girls galore," said Sam.

"We need an announcer, a voice-over, a male, and two females," Brian told us.

We studied the parts and finally decided on Elizabeth and Jill for the female roles, Sam for the announcer, Brian for the male role, and me for voice-over.

I set up two card tables to look like news desks. I sat on one side of the hall doorway, Sam sat on the other.

After we'd practiced a couple of times, we called Dad in for a sneak preview.

"Lights! Camera! Action!" said Sam, and Brian came to the doorway and stood forlornly with his hands in his pockets.

Sam: "Do you ever feel that life is passing you by because of your smile?"

Brian gave a halfhearted smile, his lips clamped tightly together. He sure looked like a loser.

Sam: "More specifically, do you feel that life passes you by because of your *teeth*? Dingy, where they should shine? Yellow, where they should gleam?"

Brian nodded ruefully, one hand over his mouth, looking sheepish.

Sam: "Do friends avoid you?"

Elizabeth and Jill walked in from the hallway, took one look at Brian, and turned their backs on him, arms folded across their chests.

Sam: "Bosses ignore you?"

Brian held up a sign saying DEMOTION.

Sam: "Strangers give you the cold shoulder?"

Elizabeth and Jill left.

Sam: "Don't just stand there, brush with The White Stuff!"

Me: "Brought to you by a subsidiary of the same company that makes your teeth brown in the first place, Smutty Smokes."

Sam: "Nine out of ten doctors . . ."

Me: "Veterinarians, perhaps . . ."

Sam: ". . . agree that The White Stuff is more effective . . ."

Me: "Than what?"

Sam: ". . . in making your teeth whiter, brighter in just ten days."

Brian smiled a full, idiotic smile, showing his teeth.

Sam: "Leading doctors . . ."

Me: "Make that, doctors leading their dogs, perhaps . . ."
I heard Dad laugh.

Sam: ". . . agree that if you use The White Stuff daily, you will notice a remarkable difference in only ten days."

Me: "A difference in what? Your teeth? Your weight? Your pocketbook?"

Sam: "The boss will notice."

Brian held up another sign saying PROMOTION.

Sam: "Friends will notice."

Jill and Elizabeth came back in and hung on to Brian's arms, looking at him adoringly.

Sam: "And you will increase your self-confidence and self-esteem."

Me: "That's all it takes, folks, and your life will be perfect. Yeah, right!"

Brian: (holding up the toothpaste tube) "The White Stuff. The *right* stuff! Never be without it."

Dad laughed and clapped. "Absolutely revolting," he said. "Great job."

We read off all the categories—incomplete data, appeal to vanity, etc.—and Dad said we had covered all the bases.

We fooled around after that. Jill and I did some variations of "Chopsticks" on the piano, and Sam had brought his camera, so he took close-ups of everybody. I guess if you're a true photographer, you take a camera everywhere. I was already getting the idea that Sam was one of the best photographers in the Camera Club. I also noticed that he hung around my place for a while after the other kids left.

"Who plays the piano here?" he asked. "You?"

I laughed. "No, my dad. He's manager of The Melody Inn. Everybody's musical in my family except me. Of course, if I used The White Stuff . . ."

Sam laughed, too. "The *right* stuff . . ."

". . . I'd be playing Chopin," I told him.

"How many in your family?" he wanted to know.

"Three. Dad and Lester and me. Lester goes to the University of Maryland. He's twenty-one. Senior year." And then, because I didn't want him to think Dad was divorced, I added, "Mom died when I was in kindergarten."

"Oh," said Sam.

"What about you?" I asked.

"Just Mom and me. She's divorced," said Sam.

I had a terrible thought that Sam might try to get his mom and my dad together, so I said, "Dad's been dating Miss Summers from school."

"Yeah?" Sam looked puzzled. "No kidding? I thought she and Sorringer were an item."

"Not anymore," I said, but didn't say anything else for fear Dad might hear us from the kitchen.

When Sam had gone, Dad ambled in eating an apple. The smell of baking bread filled the house.

"Another boyfriend?" he asked.

"Not really."

"Looks to me as though he likes you, Al."

"I guess he does. I like him, too. I mean, he's okay. But I've got Patrick."

Dad didn't say any more. Just sat down at the piano and thumbed through the pages of some new sheet music. Then he put his apple down and began practicing the Mozart sonata he'd been working on for a week. I curled up in one corner of the couch with my English assignment, but watched Dad's fingers at the keyboard.

I've got Patrick sounded so sure. So final. Maybe Dad didn't say anything because he was trying to tell me that nothing is sure. Maybe I'd been looking at life like The White Stuff commercial, as though everything wonderful would follow if only I had a mother. Suppose it wasn't like that at all? Sometimes, in fact, as Pamela would say, a mother can cause more problems than she solves. Of course, maybe Dad was looking at life that way, too, as though he had to have Sylvia Summers or nobody. Why wasn't *he* dating other women?

Well, maybe he was. I guess there was a time he and Janice Sherman went out for a while. And the summer we went to the beach, he'd been attracted to the woman in the beach house next door, I knew, but somehow that never worked out.

"Dad," I said.

"Hmmm?" He went on playing, but slightly softer so he could hear me.

"When you and Mom were married . . . did you ever swap wives with anyone?"

Dad's hands dropped from the keyboard and he turned slowly around on the piano bench. *"What?"*

"Did you ever take Mom to a dance, maybe, and swap partners and dance cheek to cheek with somebody else's wife, and then take somebody else's wife home with you?"

"Al, what on earth have you been watching on TV?" he asked.

"That's not real life?" I asked hopefully.

"Not in *this* house it isn't," he told me.

I took a deep breath and smiled. "That's all I wanted to know," I said.

8

Decision

As February turned to March, I was too busy to worry much about Dad and Miss Summers. I had let all the other priorities on my list go neglected in my obsession with Miss Summers, and now that she'd turned down Sorringer's ring, it was time to concentrate on other things.

"I don't know whether I want to be a psychologist or a psychiatrist; I'm getting to know Sam better, but I'm more confused than ever; I think I'm developing a potbelly; I haven't done much for Lester lately; and my life's a mess," I said to Pamela when she called that night.

"Yeah, tell me about it," she said wryly. Our favorite saying. We were definitely into spring slump.

The commercial had gone over well in social studies, though; Dad finished the income tax; I discovered in Camera Club that I took much better pictures of people than I did of scenes and objects, which helped confirm my feeling that I'd be happiest in a job working with people; Patrick and I had gone to the movies a couple of times; and I had long talks on Saturday mornings with Marilyn at The Melody Inn.

I can talk with Marilyn about anything. Well, almost anything. I asked her once how long she was willing to wait for Lester, and she said, "Who's waiting?" which sort of unnerved me.

"What do you and Lester talk about when you're out on a date?" I asked that first Saturday in March.

"*Excuse* me?" she said, her eyes laughing.

"I don't mean the details," I said hurriedly. "I mean, do you talk about the future or about things you've already done, or is it mostly about classes or what?"

"It's about everything," Marilyn told me, and I noticed how brown her eyes are. Brown eyes and long brown hair. She's short and thin, but not skinny—just lean, like a girl who grew up in the mountains.

"But . . . but how do you talk about the future without including each other in it? And if you include each other in it, aren't you sort of committing?"

"That's the sixty-four-thousand-dollar question, Alice," she said. "We sort of dance around it without ever resolving anything."

"Oh," I said.

Later, when I was stamping sheet music for Janice Sherman, I was thinking about how impossible it was to do anything with Sam without making Patrick jealous. I realized, of course, that if Patrick started getting interested in other girls, I'd probably be jealous, too.

"A penny for your thoughts," Janice said to me. "Do you

realize you just stamped that last sheet upside down?"

I quickly turned it right side up and did it over. "I was thinking about life," I told her.

Janice smiled. "That's a big topic. Can you narrow it down a little?"

"Love," I told her. "I was thinking about how much easier things would be if nobody got jealous. If you could just wake up in the morning and pop an antijealousy pill."

"Well, maybe things would be easier, but then, what's the point of love? Love is supposed to make you feel special, and how can you feel special if your beloved is treating other women the way he treats you?"

She had a point. But was I really talking about love? I wondered. Did I really "love" Patrick? Or just like him a lot?

"If two people just *like* each other, though, they should be able to date as many others as they want, shouldn't they?" I asked.

"*Liking* won't do it for me, Alice," Janice said, and she wasn't smiling anymore. "If a man loves me, I expect him to forsake all others, just like the marriage vows say."

Oh, boy! I thought. I was talking about Patrick and me, and she was talking about her and Dad. Do you know what love is? It's a food chain! A feeding frenzy! Janice has had a crush on Dad forever, he has a crush on Miss Summers, Miss Summers has a crush on somebody, we're not sure who . . .

On the bus Monday, I told Elizabeth and Pamela how unsettled I felt, and they said they were feeling the same way.

"Like everything's upside down," said Elizabeth.

"Inside out," said Pamela.

"Maybe it's the eighth-grade syndrome," I suggested. "Maybe it's when we're thirteen that we find out the world isn't exactly like we thought it would be."

Elizabeth sighed. "What I wish is that there could be one day of the week when things stayed absolutely the same. A day you could count on when nothing startling would happen. For that one day your life would remain peaceful and quiet."

"How about a whole week, not just a day? A whole *month,* even," said Pamela. "Sometimes I feel that if Mom doesn't come back to Dad, I won't be able to stand it."

"I sort of feel that way about Patrick—if he broke up with me," I confessed. "And yet I'm the one talking about going out with other guys. It's nuts."

I did wonder about Patrick and me. He always seemed so busy lately. He has a lot of interests—track, drums, debate team, French Club, chess—and he wonders if he can't squeeze in swim team as well. I hadn't noticed that he was interested in any other girl; he just had his life on fast-forward, that's all.

After third period, Pamela and I were in the rest room curling our hair when Elizabeth suddenly rushed in, her cheeks pink, and backed up against the wall, her arms stiffly at her sides.

"What's the matter with *you*?" Pamela asked.

Elizabeth looked both flustered and excited. "You'll never guess! Justin just stopped me in the hall and asked me to the semi-formal."

Pamela and I shrieked like a two-toned fire alarm.

"He just stopped you in the hall and asked?" I wanted to know.

"Yes!" Elizabeth was smiling now. "I said I'd go."

We squealed some more. "Elizabeth, you're the first one of us to be asked! It's wonderful!" I told her. Only I had to admit to myself that right at that moment I felt a little jealous. Patrick and I were supposed to be going together, and he hadn't said anything about the dance to me.

It was all we three girls talked about at lunch, and we sat together for the teacher recognition assembly, too. Because our school has a student recognition assembly, I guess they figure a teacher recognition ceremony is worth having, where grants and awards and stuff are announced. It's one of the most boring assemblies of the whole year, but we have to go.

There was a row of teachers sitting up on the platform, and I was pleased to see that Miss Summers was one of them. *Doubly* pleased that Mr. Sorringer wasn't there at all. Mr. Ormand, our principal, did the honors, and the seventh-grade girls' chorus provided the music.

It's really weird to be an eighth-grade girl sitting in the bleachers, looking down at the rows of seventh-grade girls, thinking how you were once short and skinny like that; flat-chested. That your voice was so high.

We listened to the teachers' names read off who had had articles published, or who'd received grants to try new projects in the classroom. The basketball coach got an award for our winning team. The art teacher got special recognition for her paintings in a Washington, D.C. gallery. Mr. Everett, the health teacher and everybody's favorite male teacher, got two different awards for inventiveness in the classroom. We clapped and cheered.

And then there were only three teachers left.

"Sylvia Summers," Mr. Ormand said, and Miss Summers smiled while Mr. Ormand read off her particular honor. Whatever it was for, I beamed.

"It's no secret to our school that Miss Summers is one of the best English teachers we have ever had," said Mr. Ormand, and we clapped and cheered again. A few of the guys whistled. It's no secret, either, that some of the guys are practically in love with her. How could they *not* be?

"And so," Mr. Ormand continued, "it's no surprise, I guess, that her fame has spread far and wide. We feel honored that although she has been offered positions in other schools, both public and private, she has always chosen to remain here. But yesterday she received an offer she couldn't refuse . . ."

I think my heart actually stopped beating. How did I seem to know that the next line would be: *She has accepted a proposal of marriage and will be leaving the teaching profession to be a wife to Ben McKinley, and stepmother to Alice.* I held my breath.

". . . so I am delighted in one way, sad in another, to announce that Sylvia Summers has been accepted as an exchange teacher in England for one year and will be leaving us in June to broaden her teaching skills in Chester, England. I know you will join me in congratulating this wonderful teacher."

The auditorium burst into applause, but I was frozen in my seat.

"Alice!" Pamela and Elizabeth cried together in dismay.

The next thing I knew I was almost tumbling over the legs of the other girls in the row to get down. With Elizabeth and Pamela, I rushed to the exit and burst out the doors into the hall, heading for the rest room.

"She's sick," I heard Elizabeth say to the teacher standing there at the door.

I hurried into the rest room—the same rest room where Elizabeth had announced her good news only a few hours before. I leaned against the towel dispenser and covered my face with my hands.

"Oh, Alice!" Elizabeth said again, putting her arms around me.

I hated Miss Summers! She had been leading my dad on! She'd been pretending to be a part of our family when she wasn't at all. She was selfish and inconsiderate—incapable, maybe, of love. But how was she going to tell Dad?

I cried bitterly, my shoulders and chest heaving as I tried to catch my breath.

There was another time I had left a school assembly—the time Mr. Ormand had announced the suicide of Denise Whitlock. At that time, Miss Summers had seen me leave and had followed me out into the hall. She had hugged me and comforted me, and I was half-expecting her to come to me now, to tell me it was all a mistake. But nothing happened. Nobody came.

There was one more period in the day, and I avoided her room, her corridor, completely. I didn't want to see her ever again. Didn't want to talk with her, call her, smile at her—nothing. She had broken my father's heart, I felt certain, and it was beyond repair. I would never forgive her! Never, ever!

Some of the kids could tell I'd been crying. Patrick met me at the bus going home and sat with his arm around me while I cried into his jacket.

"I just feel so sorry for my dad," I gulped.

"Maybe he has other girlfriends you don't even know about," said Patrick.

"Get real," I said, suddenly turning my face toward the window. Sometimes Patrick knows exactly the right thing to say, and sometimes he doesn't.

He squeezed my shoulder. "I can imagine how you feel, Alice, but it's not the end of the world. Your dad has gotten along okay so far without a wife. And I know that you wanted her in the family, but you've gotten along okay, too, and you're pretty and funny and smart."

That was the right thing to say. I snuggled against him and stayed that way till he got off at his stop. Then Pamela got off, and at our stop, Elizabeth and I walked arm in arm up the sidewalk together.

"You know, Alice," she said, "if you ever need a mom to talk mother-daughter stuff with, you can always use mine."

"Thanks," I told her, but that was impossible, I knew. How could I ever go to Mrs. Price, for example, and tell her I was envious of Elizabeth? Of her good looks and gorgeous skin and the fact that she was the first one of us three to be officially invited to the semi-formal?

Lester wasn't home yet, so I went up to my room and stood at my dresser, staring at a picture I'd taken of Dad and Miss Summers at Christmas. He was on the couch, and she was sitting on the floor in front of him. They looked so happy then. Dad's fingers were caressing her shoulder, his other hand sort of cupped over her ear. Or maybe he was stroking a lock of hair.

I pulled open my drawer and saw the little gold whistle on its gold chain that she had given me, and I started to cry all over again. If I blew it, she wouldn't come. How could she *do* this to us? *Why* did she do it?

Suddenly I sat down hard on my bed. Maybe I was to blame! Maybe my telling her that Mr. Sorringer had been

seen with another woman had made her feel that men
could simply not be trusted, Dad included, and she decided to leave the country! Or maybe she knew I was lying
and decided she could never be the stepmother of a girl
who would lie. Or maybe she believed me, but was angry
that I was a snitch!

I threw myself back on the bed in agony, staring up at the
ceiling. That was it! Just when she was feeling most in love
with Dad and a part of our family, I had messed up good,
and she wanted to get as far away from both Mr. Sorringer
and our family as possible.

That's why she refused Mr. Sorringer's diamond.

That's why she was going to England.

It was all because of me meddling in their love life, hers
and Dad's, and I was to blame for the whole thing. I
sobbed.

I wanted in the worst way to talk to Lester, but he didn't
get home till Dad had already come in and started dinner.

"Al? You home?" Dad called up the stairs.

I tried to sound normal. "Yeah, I'm studying. Need any
help?" I called back.

"No, I can manage. Dinner in about fifteen minutes," he
told me.

I washed my face and tried to powder out the red around
my eyes. When Lester came in and we sat down to eat, Dad
said, "Well, I got some rather surprising news yesterday.
Sylvia has accepted a position as an exchange teacher in

England for a year, beginning this June." And then he added, "I'm going to miss her."

Les stopped chewing, glanced at me, then back at Dad. I was afraid to speak for fear I'd bawl.

"I guess it's something she's always wanted to do, and when she got the chance, decided to take it."

"I'm sure she must be going with mixed feelings," Lester said, trying to put the best possible face on it.

Dad didn't answer.

"We heard at school," I said, knowing I had to say *something*. "They announced it in assembly. I wish she'd stay . . ." My voice quavered.

"Well, so do I," said Dad. "But it's her choice to make, not ours."

Lester went on eating, frowning down at his plate. "She ever mention this before, Dad?"

"No. She only said she liked to travel. I knew she loved England, and hoped to return for a vacation sometime, but she'd said nothing about teaching there. So naturally, it was something of a shock."

I struggled to keep tears out of my eyes. "I thought she had a good time here at Christmas!" I said. "I thought she wanted to come back again and again."

"She *did* have a good time, honey, and I think she does want to come back. But she also wants a year in England, and I'm not going to stand in her way."

I lost it then.

"Well, maybe you should!" I cried. "Maybe you should propose and tell her we'll all go with her! You could be married in England, and . . ."

"Al!" Lester barked at me from across the table, and he looked so serious that I immediately shut up.

"Al," said Dad, more gently. "I *have* asked Sylvia to marry me. Several times, in fact. So I appreciate your concern, but I'd rather handle this my own way."

I sat mutely, absorbing this knowledge, but when Dad went back to the store that evening to do inventory with Marilyn Rawley and Janice Sherman, I burst into Lester's room and threw myself, sobbing, onto his bed.

He turned around, sighed, then went on typing.

"Lester!" I wailed. "I've done something terrible and it's all my fault that Miss Summers is going to England, and I know you'll want to disown me, but I thought I was helping Dad and I wasn't."

Now he stopped typing. "Al, what did you do?"

Between tears and swallows, I told him how I'd made up a fib about Jim Sorringer, and what I'd told Miss Summers.

"Well," he said gravely, "whether this is why she's leaving or not, you still owe someone an apology."

I wiped my nose. "Dad?"

"No. Sylvia."

"I can't! *Why?*"

"Because she's the one you lied to. Technically you should apologize to Sorringer, too, but we'll assume he doesn't know about it. I want you to go out there to the phone and call Sylvia."

"I *can't,* Lester!" I wept. "I can't tell her something like that over the phone!"

"Then talk to her at school tomorrow."

"Les-ter! She could have a bunch of kids around her."

"Then tell her you're coming over, and I'll drive you."

I gaped at Lester. "You're . . . you're serious!"

"Never more serious in my life."

"Couldn't I just write her a note?"

"This is goof-up big time, Al. It's more than a note."

I walked out in the hallway as though facing my execution and slowly picked up the phone.

confession

I felt like Anne Boleyn going to the chopping block; Joan of Arc on her way to the stake. I had tried to save my father from the loneliness of widowerhood, and now I had to confess to the woman he loved that I'd lied.

"Can you tell me what you want to talk about, Alice?" Miss Summers asked when I called her.

"N-No," I wept. "I have to see you in person."

"Well, then, why don't you come right over?" she said. "Who's bringing you?"

"Lester."

"Okay. See you in a little while."

I sat silently on the passenger side of the car, not looking left or right. A white lace garter swung from Lester's rearview mirror—the garter he'd caught at somebody's wedding when the groom threw it to his buddies. Right now it seemed the most obscene thing in the world.

"I don't like that garter," I said in a small voice.

Lester reached up, slipped it off his mirror, and tossed it into the backseat. "Anything else displease you? I should change the seat covers, maybe?"

"I'm just sick of wives leaving husbands and teachers leaving schools and men swapping wives and guys catching garters. I'm sick of the whole mess. This world is one big revolving door, and I hate it."

"The world has its good days and its bad days, Al, just like you. You won't always feel this way," Lester told me.

I began to tear up again. "Les, what am I going to *say* to her?"

"The truth."

"She'll *hate* me!"

"Well, that's a chance you'll have to take," he said.

"Couldn't I just tell Dad and let him tell her?"

"He didn't lie to her; you did."

We rode some more in silence. "I'll bet you never had to do anything like this," I said bitterly.

"I sure did."

"When?"

"When Mom was still alive and we lived back in Chicago."

"You lied to Mom?"

Lester shook his head. "Aunt Sally."

I looked over at him. "What did you do?"

"Ate her goldfish."

I laughed in spite of myself. "Ate her *goldfish*?"

"All seven of them, in fact, and told her they just died."

"But why?"

"A friend dared me. We read about some college kids doing it back in the twenties, and after this kid dared me, I swallowed one of Aunt Sally's fish. Then my friend did, only he said he'd eaten a bigger one than I had, so I had to eat a larger one. Then *he* ate a larger one, and we kept trying to one-up each other until they were all gone. We just kept swallowing them down with a big glass of water. I swear I could feel one swimming around in my stomach."

"That is so gross! And Mom made you 'fess up?"

He nodded.

"Why were you afraid to tell Aunt Sally?"

"I was afraid she'd give me a laxative or something. Sal is big on purging."

That should have put me in a more cheerful mood, but by the time we reached the small house on Saul Road in Kensington, my eyes welled up again.

"Lester," I gulped. "If Dad and Miss Summers don't marry, I just won't be able to stand it."

Lester pulled over to the curb in front of Miss Summers's house and faced me. "Yes, you will, Alice," he said, and he never calls me "Alice." "You will because you'll *choose* to stand it. When Mom died I felt the way you're feeling now, only worse. I didn't think anybody could understand the way I felt. You were too young, and Dad was her husband, not her son. I decided I could either cave in or I could carry on, so I carried on, and you will, too."

I sat there thinking about that—the way our lives seemed

right then, mine and Elizabeth's and Pamela's. Pamela said she couldn't stand it if her parents didn't get together again, Elizabeth said she couldn't stand going for another pelvic . . . Lester was right. Of *course* we would stand it. We might be miserable for a while, but somehow we'd make it.

"Wait for me here, Lester," I said. "I'm not sure how long this will take."

Lester turned off the engine, turned on the radio, and settled back.

I went up the walk, then up the steps, and tapped on the door. Then I remembered the doorbell and rang that.

Miss Summers answered. She wore corduroy pants and a bulky yellow sweater. She studied me carefully as I stepped inside.

"I'll bet I know what this is all about," she said, putting an arm around my shoulder, and then I broke down. As soon as the door closed behind me, I bawled.

We sat side by side on her couch, and all I could do was cry. I was thoroughly disgusted with myself. You'd never know I was in the eighth grade. I felt more like I was in kindergarten.

"Is this about the assembly?" she asked.

I nodded and held a tissue to my nose.

"I'm really sorry you had to find out that way, Alice. I only got the news myself yesterday, so Mr. Ormand added my name to the teacher recognition list. I didn't even know I'd be up there . . ."

"You didn't know you'd been accepted as an exchange teacher till yesterday?" I asked in this teeny-tiny voice that sounded like a kitten's mew.

"No. Alice, do you want some tea while we talk?"

I nodded. Somehow it would seem easier with a cup of tea in my lap, I thought. I watched while she went to the kitchen, put two cups of water in the microwave, and returned with tea.

I thought about what she'd said, but wasn't sure I believed her. "What I came to tell you is that"—I gulped—"I lied to you. I wanted so much for you to marry Dad that . . . that when I found out you were spending New Year's Eve with Mr. Sorringer, I . . . ." Here I let out my breath and tried again. "I made up that story about seeing Mr. Sorringer with another woman. Well, not exactly, because I *had* seen him in a car with Mrs. Rollins on their way to Pizza Hut." My voice cracked a little. "I wanted you to think that if you married him, he couldn't be trusted, so I made up that story."

"Oh," she said quietly. I glanced at her sideways and saw that she had pressed her lips together. "I guess I did wonder about that some, but decided pretty quickly that it wasn't true, and guessed at why you'd done it. The truth is, I applied to be an exchange teacher last October, not since you told me about Mr. Sorringer, so the lie really had nothing to do with my decision, if that's what you're thinking."

I stared. "Last October?"

"Yes. I've always wanted to go to England again, I loved it

so when I visited once. Living there as an exchange teacher sounded as though it would be ideal. So when I read about this grant last fall, I decided there was no harm in trying. I had all the qualifications they were asking for, and I just decided that . . . well . . . with all the confusion in my life right then, maybe this would be good for me. That when I came back, things would be clearer. It's only for a year."

I looked at her in dismay. "*Only* a year! It's a whole year out of my dad's life, Miss Summers! It's a whole year you could be married!" I set my cup on the coffee table and cried in earnest.

"Oh, honey . . ." Miss Summers put her arm around me and drew me closer while I blew into my Kleenex. "This is all very grown-up stuff, but I think you're entitled to know some of it. Jim Sorringer and I have known each other for a long time. I guess we sort of assumed that we'd marry eventually, though we're both very serious about our careers.

"He went to California to finish his Ph.D., and—as you know—it was while he was gone that I met your dad and . . . and fell in love with him."

I gasped and turned to look at her. She'd actually said she loved him.

"Then why . . . ?"

"Because I'm not entirely convinced I don't still love Jim as well. I'd love to be your stepmother, to be Ben's wife, but at the same time, I have to ask myself, 'Do I know what I'm doing?' The worry has been eating at me, Alice—I've even lost some weight over it—because I don't want to make a mistake. Too many people are involved. A year away by myself just might be what I need to decide."

"What if you meet someone else over there?" I croaked, and this time she laughed.

"I think I've got more decisions than I can handle right now."

"But . . . but . . . don't you want to marry and have . . . have a baby while . . ." I never dreamed I'd be asking her anything so personal, but at this point I didn't care.

"While I can?" she asked gently. "I wish I could, but I've had a hysterectomy, Alice, so I can never have children. I guess my students are my children, and I'm happy. But I promise to come back, and whatever I decide, I know I'll want to see you first thing."

I hugged her. "I'll want to see you, too. So will Dad. And I'm sorry I told that lie."

"I am, too, but I understand why you did it. Thanks for coming over, Alice. This is woman-talk, you know. Between the two of us."

"I know."

I had felt as low as a centipede when I walked through her door twenty minutes before, and now, as I went back out again, I felt I had turned into a butterfly or something. I had just had a woman-to-woman talk with Miss Sylvia Summers. I knew something about her body none of the other kids knew. She had actually poured her heart out to me—to *me*—Alice Kathleen McKinley like . . . like I was a psychiatrist or something! I opened the car door and slid elegantly onto the seat beside Lester.

He turned off the radio. "Well?" he said, glancing over.

"You can take me home now," I said grandly.

Lester turned the key in the ignition, still looking at me. "Did you level with her, Al?"

"Completely."

"The whole truth, and nothing but the truth?"

"It's confidential, and I will protect it with my life," I said.

"I see. And is there anything else the duchess cares to share with her chauffeur?"

"Only that a year will help Miss Summers clear up her confusion, and that she's looking forward to seeing us again."

"Thank you, Miss McKinley, for your enlightening information," said Lester.

I grinned at him, and he smiled back as he turned toward the Beltway and headed home.

I did not call Elizabeth and Pamela when I got back. I was afraid I'd tell them too much. I didn't tell Dad I'd gone to see Miss Summers, either. I knew she'd told him all she'd told me, and more. When I saw my friends at school and they asked if I'd found out anything, I just said that she and Dad were very fond of each other, but that being an exchange teacher for a year was something she'd always wanted to do, and Dad wouldn't stand in her way.

How was it, though, I wondered, that Miss Summers could have had a hysterectomy and still look so gorgeous and sexy, while Janice Sherman had lost her uterus, too, and acted as though if she didn't get it or Dad or a trombone instructor or *something*, she would take a vow of crabbiness for the rest of her life?

And then I remembered reading something Dad had scribbled on the inside corner of one of our poetry books: *Happiness is wanting what you have.* Being happy with what you've got. Enjoying it, and making it all it could be, in other words. I went to the shelf to read it again, but when I opened the cover I saw it wasn't Dad's handwriting at all: It was Mom's.

something Hopeful

I felt strangely calm and quiet the rest of that week. It was as though I had been waiting all these months for the other shoe to drop–to find out whether Miss Summers would or wouldn't marry Dad. I still didn't know, but suddenly everything was on hold.

Elizabeth had said there ought to be a day each week when nothing could happen to change your life, and for now–for Dad's love life, anyway–we had a whole year. But maybe not. Maybe *Dad* would find someone else and fall in love. I had to be prepared for anything.

The point was, whatever happened, I could live with it. As Patrick said, this wasn't the end of the world. Miss Summers must have felt pretty terrible when she found out she could never have children, but she decided to live a full and happy life anyway. I'd be really unhappy for a while if she decided to marry Mr. Sorringer, but I'd get over that, too. And I knew that Dad wouldn't let it ruin his life, either. He still had Les and me.

Maybe Dad was feeling the same way, because he was

quiet, but he didn't seem as depressed. At least he knew that Mr. Sorringer wouldn't be near her, either, and he couldn't help but be glad she'd refused Sorringer's ring.

Life sort of returned to normal. In Camera Club we were practicing action shots with 400-speed film, and there were times Sam seemed to know as much as the teacher. His mom is a photographer for a weekly newspaper, he told me, so that's why he knows so much.

At Elizabeth's house, Nathan was over his colic and we were having a lot of fun—Elizabeth, Pamela, and I—trying to get him to laugh. I never knew that a baby has to practice laughing. I mean, when he laughed for the first few times, it sounded more like hiccups. He even startled himself. He'd laugh, then look around as if to say, "Where did *that* come from?"

Pamela's mom had a fight with her NordicTrack instructor and was talking about coming back home, but Mr. Jones says he doesn't want her back. Pamela came over and stayed with me for a couple of days to let them sort it out, and we played lots of board games with Lester and concentrated on just having fun. I think it helped, even though her mom and the NordicTrack guy made up again.

Meanwhile, we were learning new things at school. Mr. Kessler, in biology, brought in a bunch of frogs—dead, of course, and pickled in formaldehyde—and we had to dissect them, two people per frog. I got Sam for a partner.

"Tell me again just how knowing the difference between a

frog's stomach and spleen is going to help me in my future life," I quipped.

And Sam whispered, "I have it on good authority that this isn't biology at all. It's gourmet cooking, and after we remove the intestines, we're going to have frog legs for lunch." We laughed out loud.

We each had a long pair of tweezers and were removing organs one by one and placing them on a paper towel. I had just lifted out part of the intestines when Sam said, "Alice, would you go to the semi-formal with me?"

The intestines dropped on the paper towel, and I watched the formaldehyde stain spreading slowly across the paper.

"Don't look so startled," Sam said. "I didn't ask you to eat those or anything."

I tried to laugh, but my head whirled.

"Well, I . . . actually, I'm . . . gee, Sam, I don't know what to say," I finally blurted out. "I'm flattered, really, that you asked, but . . . well, I'm sort of going with Patrick Long."

"Just sort of?" he said. "I mean, has he asked you to the dance?"

"Well, not yet, but . . ."

"Maybe he's taking someone else."

"Oh, no. I mean, he wouldn't . . ." I looked at Sam. "*Is* he?"

"I don't know. I was just asking. Listen, though. If he *does* take someone else, I'd like you to go with me. Just let me know, okay?"

"Well, sure! But I don't expect you to wait around."

"I won't."

The rest of the day was a blur. I couldn't have told a frog's leg from a frog's lung after that. When I saw Elizabeth and Pamela later and told them, Elizabeth said, "It would be wrong to go with Sam when you belong to Patrick, Alice."

"Belong? Like a dog or something?"

"It would be preadultery, practically," she said.

I came to a stop right there in the hallway. "Preadultery? Good grief, Elizabeth, does every sin have a prefix?"

"A lot of venial sins add up to mortal sins, you know," she told me. I'll bet Elizabeth has rules that not even her priest would recognize.

But as the day went on, I decided that while I couldn't make changes in anyone else's love life, I could do something about my own. And when we got on the bus that afternoon, I sat down in one of the seats and pulled Patrick down beside me before he could go sit with his buddies near the back.

"Patrick, I have to know," I said. "Are we going to the semi-formal together or not?"

"Of course!" He looked at me and handed me a stick of gum, but I pushed it away.

"I mean, am I special to you or not?" I asked.

"What do you think? I gave you a one-pound Hershey's Kiss for Valentine's Day, didn't I? Do you think I put one in all the girls' lockers?"

"Well, if you *weren't* planning to take me to the dance, I'd decided to go with someone else."

Now he was really staring. "Who?"

"It doesn't matter, but I had to know."

"Of course I'm planning to take you. Who else would I take? I didn't think I had to ask. I just assumed . . ."

"You took me for granted, Patrick! Like I'll always be here waiting for you, faithful Alice, whether you ask me or not," I said.

Patrick got to his feet, then dramatically knelt down in the aisle on one knee and reached for my hand. The other kids stared.

"Alice, will you go to the semi-formal with me?" he asked.

I started laughing. "Yes, you nut," I said, and everybody clapped.

Lester was home when I got there, and I told him about Patrick on the bus.

"What is it about knees, Al?" he asked. "Why do women like to see men down on their knees? Subjugation? Humiliation?"

"Maybe it's about the only time a girl's taller than the guy," I told him, and Lester laughed.

Dad left shortly after dinner to go over to Miss Summers's house, and I was just going out to the kitchen to see if there was any pie left when the phone rang. I answered in the hall.

"Alice?" came a familiar voice. "How are you? I haven't talked with you in a long time."

"Crystal!" I said in surprise, and Lester, who had just sprawled out on the couch with the sports section, paused with his arms in the air. "Well . . . well, how are *you*?" I asked. "How's the bride?" Is that what you say to your brother's former girlfriend who is now married to somebody else? I was a bridesmaid at her wedding last Thanksgiving.

"Oh, I'm all right, I guess. How's eighth grade going? How was Christmas?"

"Everything's fine," I told her. "Miss Summers spent Christmas Eve and Christmas Day here with us, and we had a good time. I'm going to the semi-formal with Patrick."

"Wonderful! What are you going to wear?"

"Your bridesmaid dress, what else? I look good in green."

"It'll be perfect, Alice. You looked gorgeous."

"So did you, Crystal. You were a beautiful bride."

There was a pause. "I just wondered . . . Les wouldn't happen to be around, would he?" she asked.

I guess there was a pause on my part, too. Then I said, too quickly, stumbling over my words, "Sure. I'll get him. Just a minute . . ."

Lester was already half-standing to make his getaway, newspapers falling to the floor, and shaking his head at me, but I just shrugged and held out the phone. I'd already said he was there.

He gave me a hopeless look and took the phone, and I took his place on the couch with the newspaper, but I didn't read a word. I was listening as hard as I could.

"Well, hello," Lester said, a little too formal-sounding, I thought. "Not bad . . . yeah, about the same. Philosophy paper. Major research . . . yeah, I graduate in June, but I'm thinking of graduate school, if I can get a fellowship. What's new with you? . . . hmmm . . . hmmm . . . yeah? . . . oh . . . hmmm . . . hmmm . . ."

I didn't know what Crystal was saying, but I could tell by the tone of the *hmmms* that Crystal wasn't just talking everyday stuff.

"Now, Crystal . . . ," he said at last. "I don't know why you're telling me all this . . . yeah . . . yeah . . . but that's between you and Peter . . . hmmm . . . Crystal, that chapter of your life is over now. You've got to get on with it, and you've got to do it with Peter . . . No, I don't mean to preach, but . . ."

When Lester hung up finally, I said, "Lester, I'm proud of you."

"Anybody ever tell you you've got big ears?" he said in reply.

But I went out to the kitchen, found the last piece of chocolate pie, divided it in half, and took Lester's over to him and set it on the coffee table. "From your admiring sister," I said.

I had just eaten my half and licked the plate clean when the phone rang again. Aunt Sally.

"Hello, dear," she said. "How are things going?"

I told her that Dad was out with Miss Summers, and

Lester had been working on a paper for philosophy, that I was going to the dance with Patrick, and that I had dissected frogs in biology. I didn't think I had to tell her yet that Miss Summers was going to England.

"Oh, honey, did you know that your mother was afraid of frogs?" she said.

"She was? Frogs?"

"Anything that jumped out at her. We just got the biggest kick out of Marie. Spiders she could stand, snakes, even, anything that moved slow. But let a mouse or a roach or a frog jump out, and she would let out a scream you could hear a block away. I don't know how in the world she survived her honeymoon in a tent."

"Maybe when you're in love it doesn't matter," I said.

"When you're in love, you're deaf and blind, my dear," said Aunt Sally. "You're absolutely right."

I don't know why I asked—because she was on the phone, I guess—but I said, "How do you know when you're really, truly in love with someone, Aunt Sally?"

"Oh, my, not even the greatest thinkers of the world can agree on that," she said. "I suppose when you care about that person almost more than yourself—when you can't imagine going the rest of your life without him—you're in love."

"But . . . but what if you feel that way about two different people?"

"You're in love with *two* boys, Alice?" Actually, it was Miss

Summers I had in mind, but Aunt Sally said, "At your age you can't have too many boyfriends, dear. How can you possibly know you're in love with one unless you've tried a few others?"

"Tried? Like riding a horse or something?"

"No!" Aunt Sally said quickly. "I just mean you have to go out with lots of boys and see how you're alike and how you're different. Listen, dear, I really called to say that Carol has a conference in Washington, D.C., next month, and I thought I might come with her and visit you while she attends meetings. I just wondered if it would be convenient. It would be four days the third week in April. Could you ask your dad to call me?"

"Sure," I said.

"And tell him I'll cook some of his favorite dishes as a treat—Marie's recipes," she said.

It would be a treat just seeing my suave, sophisticated cousin Carol again, I knew that.

The next day at school I stopped by the office to check on spring vacation, to see if it fell during the week Aunt Sally and Carol would be in town. Mr. Sorringer was standing by the file cabinet behind the attendance desk, talking with Mrs. Rollins.

"Her eighty-first birthday! You can't just send your mother a card without a note in it, Jim!" the secretary was saying. "If I was eighty-one and my son didn't bother to write me a letter, I'd disown him!"

Mr. Sorringer threw up his hands. "You're looking at the wrong man, Barbara. I don't do letters. I was the only kid expelled from summer camp because he wouldn't write home. I'll call. I'll send candy and flowers, but I don't do letters."

I forgot why I had gone to the office. I turned and walked back out with a smile as wide as a ruler on my face. Miss Summers would be in England for a whole year, and Mr. Sorringer didn't do letters.

My dad did letters. My dad wrote such wonderful love letters that Mom gave up wealthy, debonair Charlie Snow, according to Aunt Sally, and fell for Dad in a big way.

I stepped out into the empty corridor and thrust one fist triumphantly in the air.

"Yes!" I said, and set off to face whatever was coming next.

The club of Mysteries cats are always up to something!

JOIN THE CLUB AND READ ALL OF THEIR ADVENTURES BY

PHYLLIS REYNOLDS NAYLOR!